AWAKEN

Maggie Sunseri

QUESTION
EVERYTHING

Maggie Sunseri

Maggie Sunseri
PO Box 1264
Versailles, Kentucky 40383
www.maggiesunseri.com

Publisher's Note: This is a work of fiction. Names, characters,
places, and incidents are a product of the author's imagination.
Locales and public names are sometimes used for atmospheric
purposes. Any resemblance to actual people, living or dead, or
to businesses, companies, events, institutions, or locales is
completely coincidental.

Book Layout ©2014 BookDesignTemplates.com
Cover design by Mike Sunseri
Edited by Heather Sunseri

AWAKEN/ Maggie Sunseri. -- 1st ed.
ISBN 978-1-943165-01-8

For those who are awake.
For those who see the flaws in the system.
For those who aren't afraid to speak up for what's right.
You are my muse.

Chapter One

....

"During my years of adolescence I lost my way. I defied authority by breaking the Council's rules, lied compulsively, disrespected my parents, and even talked of leaving Oportet. My bad decisions were silly, and in a harsher sense, they were also evil and dangerous.

"As I have grown older, I have come to realize these things, and I will now use my wisdom to help children like you to not fall into dangerous traps like I did. My parents, the Council, and teachers have all helped me to realize the wonderful place to live and prosper is, in fact, where we are now. Oportet has given us a beautiful gift—a beautiful life. Those outside our society lie, cheat, and even brutally murder for money and a sick form of pleasure. The world is in rubble behind our gates—the people are narcissists and sociopaths, lacking any form of happiness or purpose. I am just thankful that I have now accepted the right way in this broken world.

"You must continue to adhere to all of the Council's rules. Each and every one of them is extremely important to your well-being and protection."

I smiled sweetly after the last words of my introductory speech. Before exiting the stage, I cast a glance toward the adults in the back of the auditorium. Head Councilman Tomlinson gave me a nod of approval, while the rest of the council members kept their usual stern and businesslike look plastered on their faces. My parents both met my gaze and gave me encouraging smiles. That wasn't my usual testimony, but the Council asked me to prepare the condensed version.

I focused all of my energy on moving my feet forward, trying to keep myself from toppling over. I felt every inch of my body shaking, and I could hardly believe I had just spoken in front of that many people without passing out. I swallowed and eyed the seat backstage meant for me. I was vaguely aware of the din of the clapping audience fading out behind me as I collapsed into my chair.

My introduction was just enough to lead the children into the annual Oportet Day speech at the middle school level. Oportet Day was our society's day of pride; it was a day to appreciate what the Council had given us. From backstage, I watched as Tomlinson made his way to the platform as the anthem died out. It was tradition for the Head Councilman to deliver speeches at each of Oportet's schools.

The high school speech was harsher in content, but not by much. Being seventeen, I had just graduated from school and was beginning my gap year activities—the activities designed to plan my future and my role in Oportet. It was certainly stressful. The Council was promising a bright future for me if I continued to share my frightening testimony against rebellion.

I shuddered as I remembered myself actually considering leaving my family, my home. After intense guidance sessions with the Council, and after my accident, I found my way again.

Our society is the only source of light, love, and order. It baffles me why anyone would choose to live anywhere else. The fall of the American government created chaos. In the outside world, people had resorted to living like savage rats— feeding off of each other to survive. Oportet, on the other hand, was a civilized, rich society created for the sole purpose of safety. Everyone here had a role to play.

"Hey, sweetheart." My mother's voice jolted me out of my trance and back to the present. "Luna, you sounded wonderful up there. Your father and I are very proud."

Getting up from my chair, I grinned and wrapped my arms around her as she pulled me in for a hug. "Thank you. Speaking in front of children is much different than adults. I just thought it was really important that they get the message." I didn't want anyone to question Oportet's way and purpose like I had; it had caused too much stress and pain for my family and friends—not to mention what it had cost me.

"Well, you did the right thing," Father said as he came to stand with us. "And I just wanted you to know that your testimony has also helped this family tremendously, as I have just been offered a position as an adviser to the Council."

Mother and I offered our congratulations and joy for this huge step in the right direction for our family. This promotion meant our income would increase as well as our political influence. Father had held a minor job in the law enforcement branch of our government, so being one of the select advisers to the Council was a major upgrade.

A sudden shift in the air made me glance over my Father's shoulder. That's when I saw him. My knees almost failed me, and I couldn't breathe.

My parents, completely unaware of my sudden panic, walked off to converse with the other councilmen and their families.

Something resonated deep inside when the boy appeared in my line of vision. He was leaning against a wall, staring at me. His messy dark hair matched his obsidian-colored eyes, which cut right through to my soul.

Who was he? I blinked, then caught my breath. He wasn't just staring at me—his eyes were narrowed at me in an intense glare. What was his problem? I suddenly felt sick to my stomach, the wave of nausea making me want to vomit.

I looked away, hoping he'd leave. But he didn't change his stance or speak to me. I had to get out of there. But the strange boy was leaning against the wall right next to the door leading to the parking lot. Taking a deep breath, I stood and crept toward the door, wondering if he'd stop me. Passing him, I gulped and looked down at the ground, quickly exiting the building.

The daylight struck me so brightly that I squinted for a few seconds, the summer heat making me even queasier. I made it a few yards before I had to stop, grateful that I appeared to be alone in the lot. I clutched my stomach as I leaned over, bile churning within me. Weakly, I collapsed on the ground, burying my head in my shaking hands. I closed my eyes and concentrated on breathing deeply, forcing my clenched body to relax.

I don't normally get panic attacks, but my hands were shaking uncontrollably, and a cold sweat broke out across my neck. Then I remembered—my little sister Megan hadn't attended today's speech because of the flu. Afraid I had suddenly come down with the same illness, I needed to get home.

My neighborhood was just across the road from the middle school. Because of the societal holiday, I doubted the roads would be too busy. Gaining the strength to stand up, I walked along the edge of the parking lot until I felt a hand on my shoulder. I jumped and spun around.

It was the boy with the cold, unforgiving eyes.

"Um...can I help you?" I mumbled, my voice shaky and unsure. He looked pained, continuing to stare into my eyes. I squirmed free from his hand and stepped back.

"Luna..." He shook his head and smiled in a humorless way that sent chills down my spine. There were dark circles under his bloodshot eyes, and a hard edge to his features. "No. This was a mistake. I don't think you can." And with that, he turned on his heels and walked away, leaving me staring at his back with an elevated heartbeat.

That was weird...really weird. I shook my head. Maybe my case of the flu was severe enough that I'd just hallucinated the entire exchange.

~~~~~

"You feel fine, but I'm going to get the thermometer just to be sure," Mother said as she headed to the medicine cabinet, her straight, red ponytail swaying behind her.

I lay on our living room couch, watching the same documentary that ran every holiday since before I was born. I tried to concentrate on the program's testimonials from those who came to Oportet from the Outside and had their lives change for the better, but my attention kept wandering back to the mysterious boy in the parking lot.

Mother handed me the thermometer and waited to see if I had a fever. I swept my sweaty hair off my face and took deep breaths to slow my racing heart.

The thermometer beeped with the final temperature. "It's ninety-nine point eight degrees," I said in a small voice. Mother sighed and took the thermometer from me. I caught her rolling her eyes at the TV screen, noticeably bothered by the glorification of Outsider immigrants. My parents were very opinionated on that subject.

"That's a shame. Megan's flu started around that temperature, and then shot up rapidly within hours. I'm sorry, I know you were looking forward to your Occupational Guidance Session." After placing the thermometer back, she headed upstairs to break the news to Father. My parents were looking forward to my OGS far more than I ever would.

The truth was that I was perfectly content with opting out of the meeting. It was the meeting to help plan my future, and I honestly had no idea what that future was. Every occupation I had considered began to sound less and less appealing as time passed by. I wasn't ready to head down any career path, but everyone else was stepping on my heels and pushing me forward.

As I was stressing, an image of the boy flashed in my mind again. I furrowed my brows in concentration. Did I know him? He knew my name, so we must have met sometime. My mind came up blank. I still had not ruled out the possibility that I had imagined him, especially because I knew virtually everyone in Oportet. Yet another part of me feared he was a part of the memories I had lost forever—during my "rebellious" phase. I suddenly wished I could see him again, just so that I could figure out this mystery.

Chapter Two

··

"How about we just skip this stupid project," Jasper Williams suggested.

I narrowed my eyes. That would mess up my perfect grades for sure. Less than a perfect school career meant a less than perfect future.

"Don't worry, princess. I was just joking."

The dark-haired, dark-eyed boy was leaning over the table towards me, so close that it was definitely popping my personal bubble. I leaned back in my chair, putting distance between us.

"You're hilarious. We better get started soon because Jenna and I have somewhere to be after school, and I want to know what we have to do before class ends." I swore that if he caused me any trouble at all with this assignment I would go straight to Mrs. Lawrence and demand a new, more fitting partner.

I almost felt sorry for him, though. I never saw anyone making an effort to talk to him or even offer a friendly smile. This was expected, of course—Jasper was an Outsider. This was his first year at our high school.

He smirked and ruined my leaning-back-in-my-chair maneuver by inching forward even more. I became aware of everything about him in that moment—the perfect messiness of his hair, the constant humor in his eyes, and the infuriating way his smile made me want to smile, too. I cleared my throat and began to read the research prompt.

"Shit," I muttered when I saw that part of the assignment was visiting the museum.

I wasn't quite sure when I had started breaking the rule against obscenities, but I noticed that most of the kids in high school also ignored the rule. I had even heard some adults defy it. My parents blamed any sort of corruption like this on the Outsiders—the people who lived beyond our walls before deciding to become citizens of Oportet.

"What is it?" Jasper snatched the paper from my hands, smirking once more when I shot him a death glare. His eyes scanned the page, and I watched as the corners of his mouth tipped upward like there was something humorous about a research prompt. "You know what this means, don't you?" he said finally. I quickly removed my gaze from his mouth and looked out the classroom window.

"What?" I asked. He was now drumming his fingers on the table, and I refrained from smacking them quiet.

"That we have a date. Since it was assigned by a teacher, I'm sure you will attend," he mocked.

I suppressed a smile, not wanting to give him the satisfaction of knowing that I found his clever insult amusing. "Whatever. It just can't be tonight."

Jasper glanced up at the clock, and then started to pack up his backpack, mere seconds left before the bell rang. "Of course not. We wouldn't want to interfere with the princess's agenda."

I rolled my eyes and stood from my seat. I did not enjoy being called a princess. The rest of the class was catching on now, collecting their things as they wrapped up planning with research partners.

"Would you be able to meet me Saturday? At noon?" I asked in a less than interested tone.

Jasper looked up at me and seemed to mentally scan through his weekend plans. "Yeah, that will work. I just need your phone number in case something comes up."

That was actually a good idea—in case we needed to do some of the project over the phone. Oportet only allowed certain modes of technology, but home phones were permitted. I had once overheard an Outsider describe what he called cell phones, which were personal, portable telephones, and it made me wonder why the Council would ban such a convenient tool.

Jasper and I exchanged house numbers as the bell rang, and I swore it looked like he was enjoying this assignment more than he should have been.

Chapter Three

....

I woke up in my bed drenched in sweat, with an awful headache and nausea. I hated being sick more than anything. It made me feel so useless and weak.

I remembered my dream in a startling level of vivid detail. It actually didn't feel like a dream at all... and the lab partner—Jasper—was the boy I had seen yesterday. I wished I could have stayed in my dream world longer. It was familiar and comforting to just be with this strange and fascinating boy. It actually felt a little *too* familiar...

I sat up, stunned: It was a memory.

The neurosurgeons had all said that any memory I had lost to my accident was gone for good. Why would they tell my parents something so extreme if it had the possibility of not being true? I was both relieved and scared that I might regain my memories.

What if I remembered something about my rebellious year that I didn't want to remember? In a way, my accident had helped me recover from my acts of disobedience. Not recalling the dark things I had said and thought sped up my counseling sessions with the Council and my road back into the standards of Oportet. I had to admit that it was a shame that my senior year was an empty canvass, especially since I took a lot of classes pertaining to occupational exploration.

So that was where I knew Jasper from—we had classes together my senior year of high school. Though, that didn't exactly help me figure out why he was acting so strange in the parking lot. Maybe I would get to see him again so he could explain. That is what I was trying to convince myself: that I needed to see Jasper again only because he could help me with my cloudy memories, and not because of this internal longing for his presence that felt both foreign and natural to me at the same time. Something odd was going on with my memories, and somehow this boy I thought I had never seen before had everything to do with it.

It took me a while to pull myself out of bed and slip on some comfortable clothing. By the time I had reached the kitchen, Mother was the only one still home. She was sitting at our quaint kitchen table sipping her usual dose of green tea. She looked up from her paperwork when she heard me approach, her eyes softening.

"Oh, honey, you look terrible!" She set down her tea and hurried to the medicine cabinet, presumably for flu medicine.

"I *feel* worse," I mumbled as I plopped down in a chair in front of her. I swallowed down the pills and thought of how to tell her about the miracle of my remembrance.

"How did you sleep last night?" She sat and continued her work.

"Well, something very strange happened."

Mother knitted her brows as she looked up to meet my eyes, but remained silent.

"I kind of remembered something from before the accident."

Something flashed in her eyes—excitement, maybe—and her hand tightened ever-so-slightly around her mug. "Really?" She raised a brow, waiting for me to elaborate.

I opened my mouth, about to tell her the entire memory, but something stopped me. "It was just a random memory from one of my first days of senior year."

"And you're sure it wasn't just a dream?"

"Yes, of course. It felt so real. And a lot lined up with what I know happened—like my teacher Mrs. Lawrence, and my last block being science." Why wasn't I mentioning Jasper? It was like someone had locked that section of my mind and hidden the key from my mouth.

"It is absolutely impossible for you to have remembered something that you lost from the accident. The neurosurgeons expressly told us that it just couldn't happen. You must have just imagined it, or it wasn't a memory that you had lost. The human mind works in unexplainable ways sometimes." Mother nodded and smiled like she was proud to have made sense of the situation.

Was it possible? It seemed unlikely that something so vivid could have been a dream, but even more unlikely that what I dreamt last night could've been a memory I had never lost. It just didn't add up. I would have recognized Jasper in the parking lot or backstage, wouldn't I have? But after that dream—*memory*—I felt like I had uncovered something I thought was lost forever.

But what did I know? I should believe what the neurosurgeons and my parents were telling me and write off any thoughts of my own. I wouldn't want to seem disobedient or untrusting of Mother's superiority. I had broken far too many of Oportet's rules in my lifetime, and they were all broken within the memories I had lost. I had to remember: My accident was a *blessing*.

"I guess you're right. It must have been my mind playing tricks on me."

Mother let out a breath and took a sip of her tea. "Of course, darling. Remember to come to me if you have any other questions, okay?" She searched my eyes for a moment, and then her shoulders relaxed as she sat back in her chair.

"I will."

Mother's face calmed slightly as she scribbled down notes. Her body language was enough to let me know that this conversation was both over and a waste of her time. She worked as a secretary for the Council, and was constantly filing paperwork—even on the weekends. I was disappointed in myself for bothering her first thing in the morning, drawing her away from her work. I gave my head a little shake. This case of the flu was screwing with my mind.

~~~~~

The medicine kicked in about halfway through the book I was reading about the founding of Oportet, and I immediately felt my body cooling. As I turned the pages, I became more and more disinterested. My mind floated elsewhere, and no matter how hard I tried, I could not stop thinking about the mysterious boy who now haunted my dreams.

Jasper.

Even with my brain running at full capacity, I simply couldn't figure out what was so important about him. I traced buried memories from the summer before senior year, which produced a wave of strong emotions: despair and this unmistakable feeling of dread that weighed me down, suffocating me anytime I tried to remember the events of last year.

And still, when it came to Jasper? Nothing.

Every single file in my mind was completely void of Jasper. Was that even his name? Or did my subconscious mind just make that up, along with the rest of the dream? There was only one way to find out, and it scared the hell out of me.

I had to somehow track this boy down and ask him. There were a great many problems to this plan. Like the fact that the last time he saw me he looked at me like I did something to royally piss him off. Or he may not be a part of my past at all. Yet, even with all of the difficulties presented, the internal forces that needed me to find him and get the truth were not letting up, and I almost didn't want them to.

~~~~~

"Jenna would like you to call her," Father announced. At the verge of sleep, I jolted up at the sudden burst of noise.

"Okay," I responded after letting out a loud yawn. After a few more moments of resting, I groggily struggled out from beneath my cozy blankets and shuffled to the upstairs phone.

The hallway was surprisingly dark for that early in the day. I battled with the multitude of switches on the wall until I found the right one. I squinted as the entire hallway was illuminated with a blinding light. I groaned as I continued down the hall, stopping to notice the time on the grandfather clock.

It was 10:40 PM. That explained my growling stomach and quiet home. I must have fallen back asleep after Father came in. I retreated back down the hall, and then paused when I heard strained, frantic voices from my parent's room. I knew better than to eavesdrop, but something about the tone of Mother's voice made me freeze in my tracks.

"I just didn't know what to do, or how to handle it! I know you talked with him and he confirmed everything we already knew, but...oh, I don't know, David! It just seemed different, so concerning...what if—"

"Jennifer. You know that's impossible." My father's insistent voice made me cringe from the other side of the door. Whatever they were discussing was private, and I was definitely intruding. I scurried back to my room, wondering for the fifth time today what was wrong with my common sense.

Everything felt different as I lay in the warmth of my bed. My mind fully alert, all I could do was absently trace my fingers over the intricate patterns woven into my comforter. Even in the dark, I envisioned the familiar floral designs etched into the fabric: the patterns that had been consistent since I could barely talk. It was nice to have something, even something as insignificant as a piece of fabric, that didn't change.

I had always been afraid of change. It haunted me, tested me, and made me question things I had never thought to question before. Maybe the reason it had always frightened me was because change was full of the unknown. I never knew how things were going to change, I just knew that they would, and that scared me more than anything else in the world.

I knew that change was necessary in order to evolve, but in Oportet, too much was frowned upon. There were standards that had to be met, standards that made Oportet what it was. Oportet gave lives meaning. Change screwed me over when I went from being a model citizen, never questioning authority and always doing as I was told, to a disobedient nightmare. *Change almost ruined my life.*

As I continued to trace my comforter and stare at the moon through my open curtains, the thought of change seemed nothing short of appalling. Change was dangerous, a pathway that only led to destruction.

Chapter Four

....

"I t's Luna's turn to wash the dishes," Megan announced as she stood from the table.

"And where are you going, young lady?" Father asked. Megan pointed to her textbooks lying idly on the coffee table and sighed. Father nodded in approval. "Sounds like a great idea. If I get any negative emails about your grades again, you'll be forbidden from seeing your friends for the rest of the school year."

"What? Dad! It's the second week of school." Megan threw her arms up in protest. Mother and I exchanged glances as we watched this father-daughter scene unfold.

"Megan, you had a major problem last year, and I don't want it repeating. What is Rule Fifty-Seven?" This was one of Father's favorites when dealing with Megan.

"Students will put forth the utmost effort in anything pertaining to his or her education; nothing short of academic excellence..." Megan faded out, deciding she'd said enough. Father nodded and let her stalk off to study.

"So how are your classes going, Luna?"

I had just stuffed my mouth with a bite of salad. After some furious chewing and swallowing I could finally talk without flashing my parents with half-chewed greens. "Fine. I'm not so excited about my science research project, though. I have to go to the Science Museum tomorrow." I cleverly avoided referring to Jasper. I did not know how my parents would react to me having to spend time with someone like him. They were more closed-minded than others in our society.

"Sounds like fun. So do you think you might like to do something with science later in life?" Mother hinted not so subtly.

Just thinking about being some sort of scientist for the rest of my life made me cringe. So wasn't happening. "No, not really. I don't think science is my...calling." That was the most courteous way I knew how to say it.

Father's eyes narrowed. "And what is it you are leaning toward?"

I stared down at my plate and fiddled with the tassels on my placemat. "I like writing," I blurted. Mother and Father traded glances. Father opened his mouth as if to say something, shook his head, and then closed it.

"Writing what, exactly?" Mother finally asked.

"I don't know. Whenever we have to write an essay for class, I always get the highest grade. I really enjoy writing down my thoughts and opinions on things." I winced at my choice of words.

Writing for fun was forbidden, especially opinion writing—unless for academic purposes, of course. Being a writer was one of the least prestigious occupations. Any creative occupation was. Working for the Council, writers notified the public of any special announcements or information through the Oportet Journal, wrote textbooks, composed rulebooks with special explanations for the younger grades, and a select few privileged writers had the permission to write historical novels or Meaningful Novels. The Meaningful Novel's purpose was to remind the people of Oportet why we have it right—the way we live our life, the condemning of the Outside, and the reason we were here to live our lives.

These novels also included powerful testimonies of Outsiders entering Oportet who had finally realized the meaning of life or biographies of councilmen and other past or present influential members of Oportet.

"Being any sort of writer," Father all but spit the word at me, "would be settling beneath you. You have worked too hard in school to earn less than a grocery store clerk." Father had a way with saying things bluntly. I knew what kind of job my parents truly longed for me to have—they dreamed of me following in their footsteps and working within the government.

"But...what if I wrote Meaningful Novels?" My words were struggling to latch on to something. The hole was already too deep. I looked over at Mother for some help, but she looked away.

"It's a bit too late to be making that kind of decision. You would have had to be going to all kinds of workshops and classes in the Council's building to be something like that. Don't tell me that being a writer is the only occupation you have considered." He crossed his arms and drew his eyebrows together.

I swallowed under his scrutiny. "No, of course not. I just don't know what I want to be yet. You caught me by surprise." Mother gave me a tentative smile, and Father's facial muscles relaxed.

"Once you have given it some thought, I would love to hear some of your ideas. Don't forget how well you do in your government classes," Father hinted. And with that he exited the room, leaving Mother and me sitting at the table.

"I'm sorry if you feel we're pressuring you, but your future is important to us, and we want to give you the best guidance we can to help you succeed." She reached out to rest her hand on my shoulder. "Go wash the dishes, and maybe later we can play some of those board games Megan got for her birthday."

Halfway through doing the dishes, I heard the phone ring. Interrupting me mid-thought, the noise startled me to the point where I lost my hold on the slippery dinner plate. I watched helplessly as it fell, and then shattered on the yellow tiles.

"Shit," I muttered absently, my heart thumping in my chest. The plates we had used that night were my late grandmother's. I ran my soapy hands through my hair as I assessed the damage. I hoped with all my strength that it didn't leave a mark on the floor. "Shit, shit, shit." Before I could bend down to pick up the pieces of glass, Mother was suddenly in front of me.

In one swift movement, her hand collided with the side of my face. A burst of pain flooded my head, and I felt myself lose balance. I stumbled, reaching my hands up to cradle the part of my face she had struck. Shards of glass pierced the bottoms of my feet. I slowly lifted my gaze from my feet, now drenched in blood, to Mother's face.

"How dare you blatantly ignore a rule!" she roared. "This is why your Father and I detest allowing you and Megan to be in the same school as the children of Outsiders. You are lucky it was me who heard you say such an obscene word! If I ever hear a word like that leave your mouth again, you will be severely punished."

I stared at her helplessly.

"It will do you well to remember that the Council's rules are the glue that holds this society together and the only thing that makes us better than the filthy creatures that dwell behind our walls. Do you understand me?" Mother's entire body shook with rage, her face tinted an unnatural shade of red.

"I—I understand," I croaked. Surges of pain erupted from the bottoms of both of my feet, drawing attention away from the numb, stinging sensation on my face.

Mother closed her eyes, seemingly calming herself. When she spoke next, her voice was more leveled. "Clean up this mess. I don't want to hear you speak for the rest of the night." She glared at me for one more moment before turning on her heel and stomping away.

I felt hot tears running down my cheeks as I stood, frozen. Frustrated with myself, I wiped the moisture from my face. Crying showed weakness; and I was by no means weak.

Chapter Five

....

I woke up shaking. Heat radiated off of me in waves, and as I shifted under the covers, I could feel my clothes clinging to my body. I tried to sit up, but my weak muscles and vertigo sent me falling backward against my pillows once more. My mouth was dry, making my sole thought how I could get a glass of water without getting out of bed.

For a while, I simply stared at the ceiling. My eyes followed each crack, and I even attempted to count every imperfection in the light yellow paint—anything to keep my mind from assessing last night's memory.

I could no longer pretend that it was anything less. It was like I had a book with missing pages, and when I found a page, I knew it belonged in the book—because it fit. Each page was adding to the story, and it was beginning to scare me less and less. Somehow, finding the missing pieces of my memory was like stitching myself back together after being torn apart by some freak accident. I was beginning to want—no, *need*—to stitch myself back together again. Not just the good parts, but the bad parts, too.

I knew that before the accident I had gone against everything Oportet stood for, but I hated relying on the accounts of others instead of my own. I was confident that having the rest of the story would not alter my current state of mind. It would only strengthen my faith that living in Oportet was the only true way to live my life.

Yet, even with these thoughts swirling around in my head, I could not draw myself away from the fact that Mother had acted so harshly towards me. I recounted the coldness in her eyes as she told me to clean my mess up—my ripped, bloody skin included. How had I extracted each miniscule piece of glass from my feet? I had deserved all that had been given to me, hadn't I? After all, I *had* broken a very clear rule.

My family had treated me like royalty since the accident. The Council had taken a special interest in my story of how I recovered from a rough patch during my teenage years and realized the error of my ways. They had given me special opportunities ever since to share my story—and help out my family in the process. It landed my father a promotion, and almost guaranteed me a well-paying job.

Finally I couldn't stand the heat enveloping my body anymore, so I crawled out of bed and began my trek to the kitchen. I wobbled down the dark hallway, pausing to listen for signs of any other member of the household's presence. The house was silent except for the ticking of the grandfather clock.

I steadied myself against the banister as I made my way down the steps. My bare feet met the cold, wooden surface with caution: the feeling of glass piercing my skin not entirely out of my mind. I even had the urge to examine the soles under lighting to see if there were any scars.

After consuming my much-needed dose of flu medicine and cold water, I collapsed into a chair and propped my left foot on my lap, followed by my right.

Sure enough, both feet had an array of faint, pinkish markings. I took in a sharp breath as I placed my foot back onto the tan carpet.

I had decided with a startling sense of certainty to keep the news of my remembrance to myself for now. I tried to justify my reasons for breaking Rule Forty-Seven—*Children shall never keep anything from his/her parents or authority figures*—but in the end I just had to accept that I had no good reason for this level of disrespect. And the funny thing was, as much as I wanted to feel bad about that, the need to keep this secret to myself overpowered the majority of my guilt.

"I heard that I gave you the flu," Megan said as she passed me on her way to the medicine cabinet. "I thought it was terrible for me to be missing my first week of eighth grade, but it must be even worse for you."

I furrowed my brows and gave her a questioning look.

"You know, your first Occupational Guidance Session?" She turned away to cough like she was dying. I was *not* looking forward to that symptom.

"Oh! Yeah...it's pretty terrible. This is the worst case of the flu I've ever had, so thanks a lot," I joked.

She smiled as she plopped a watermelon cough drop in her mouth. "Anytime." She sat down across from me with her make-up work in hand. I flicked her arm with as much force as I could muster, laughing when she let out a little squeal.

"You're such a little brat, Megan." I was incredibly thankful that my relationship with my sister wasn't tarnished by my pre-accident behavior. If it weren't for Megan and Jenna, my best friend, I didn't know how I would've held it together.

Jenna told me that I had slammed the door on our friendship last year—something I had no recollection of—and she still welcomed me back with open arms. That's what a best friend was for: forgiving even the worst transgressions.

"I really don't feel like doing this stuff," Megan whined.

I rolled my eyes and gave her a pointed look.

"What? It's not like you have the right to say anything—you're in your gap year!" She let out a huff and reluctantly started scribbling in a notebook.

"Yeah. I'm pretty great, aren't I?"

She narrowed her eyes at me and pressed her lips together in a thin line. Her long red hair was tucked behind her ears—the hair that she shared with Mother, while Father and I shared dark brown.

I patted her head as I made my way to the kitchen, dodging her attempt to swat my hand. Because I'd fallen asleep so early in the day, I had managed to go a full sixteen hours without food. My stomach let out a growl to confirm my hunger.

I dropped bread into the toaster and opened the refrigerator to retrieve the strawberry jam. I saw a figure in my peripheral and turned my head to meet Mother's gaze.

"How did you sleep, Luna?" She was scanning my face nervously. I spread jam on my toast, turning my back to her, the memory of last night still vivid in my mind.

"It was great. I think being sick has given me more sleep than I've had my entire life." When I turned with my plate in hand, she was right in front of me.

My stomach churned as I tried to act normal. We were both standing in the exact spot as the memory. I could almost feel the pain enveloping my feet as they were impaled with the many pieces of glass, and the stinging of my face when Mother's hand collided with my cheek. I took a deep breath.

"Honey, are you all right? You're very pale."

I managed a small smile. "I'm fine. Just sick." I shrugged. My hands tightened around the plate as she moved closer. In my mind I was seeing two different scenes unfolding: The scene from the past, and the scene in the present.

Each version of Mother lifted her hand, and I jerked backward, slamming my side into the open cabinet door. My grip on the plate loosened, and I struggled to catch it before it hit the ground. My hand grazed the tip of the glass just before it tumbled to the yellow tile.

I took in a sharp breath as my head spun. Mother was staring at the pieces of glass and the smeared toast with jam strewn out in front of us with her mouth open.

She raised her head to look at me, and all I could see was fear swimming in her big green eyes.

~~~~~

When I was just a little girl, I would always flee to my aunt's house after getting into trouble. Aunt May took me into her warm home filled with the scent of fresh-picked flowers, and she held me until I could calm down and tell her how I had misbehaved. It always baffled me how she could be so calm after I confessed the breaking of a rule—how she could just stroke my hair and whisper that everything would be okay.

Aunt May was ten years younger than Mother, and the two very rarely acted like sisters. They went through the motions at family dinners and acted polite while in each other's presence, but anyone could see that there was something off with the way they looked at each other.

My family knew where I was when I fled to Aunt May's. She would call them and let them know that I was all right, and knowing whom she was talking to, I would burrow under her blankets and cry harder. Then she would curl up next to me and tell me stories. It was our little secret. Storytelling was forbidden unless it came from the Council's elite writers, but Aunt May repeatedly broke the rule for me. She was the only one who had ever broken a rule for me.

Her words drew me far away from Oportet. They rolled off her tongue with such beauty and captivation—her words alone could convince me that fantasy was reality. I had no recollection of what most of her stories were about, but they were insane in the most thrilling ways.

As I grew older and was taught the contents of *Oportet's Official Rulebook*, I learned that fiction was dangerous. I became overwhelmed with guilt at our secret. I felt awful when I longed to hear Aunt May pull me out of reality and into a completely different world, and even worse when I let her continue breaking the rule for *me*. I still could not wrap my head around that truth. Aunt May not only broke the rule in front of a child, but *for* the child. It was her way of comforting me—but it was wrong.

I had no recollection of Aunt May's death. Her funeral. The last words we exchanged. *Nothing.*

After my accident, I felt great—aside from the headaches—but after my parents and Head Councilman Tomlinson explained what had happened pre-accident, I was so thankful that I had a clean slate. It didn't matter how many memories were lost in the process if it meant that I was back to normal.

As I began to regain those memories, I was struck with a feeling of loss. I couldn't even recall my own aunt's death. There was something terribly wrong with having this gaping hole in my head—this hole that threatened to consume me.

After I caused the scene in the kitchen, I fled just as I had in my childhood, but instead of to Aunt May's, I fled without a destination. I hastily pulled on some tennis shoes and rushed out the door, ignoring Mother's voice begging me to stay and warning me that I was too sick to go outside.

I found that the fresh air was much better for my case of the flu than the suffocating walls of the house. My muscles protested against movement, and I had to slow my pace to a painfully slow walk. I followed the main road until I reached a dirt path. The narrowness of the path made it obvious that it was meant for walking, but where it could possibly lead to was puzzling. The trail disappeared into the array of trees that could barely be considered a forest, but everyone called it that anyway.

No one went into the forest. I almost turned away and continued my aimless trek along the road, but a nagging feeling crept its way to my feet, pulling my body forward.

I cautiously dragged myself along the trail, stopping every so often to scan the area around me. I was too paranoid...the forest frightened me to the bone. It was something about the way everything was so much darker, and I was constantly among the contorted limbs of tall, eerie masses. The shadows haunted me, the birds' sharp, black eyes glared at me from above, and each twig-snap sounded like a creature closing in on me. Branches reached out, threatening to drag me into the earth and become lost in the darkness forever.

Sunlight crept through the spaces between the tops of trees, filling me with warmth and confidence. A flutter of familiar feelings erupted inside me, and I pushed all of my flu symptoms to the back corner of my mind as I walked on for another ten minutes. A voice inside my head told me to break apart from the path at one point, and as crazy as it sounded, I listened without hesitation. Somehow, I knew where I was going; but I didn't at the same time. It was like the half of my brain that knew was only telling me how to get there, but not what the place was or why it seemed so significant.

I stopped when I reached a small clearing, and what looked like an abandoned playground. Difficult-to-identify emotions overwhelmed me. What was left of the swing-sets and slides were overrun with vines and moss. Among all of the green, there was a single bench, completely cleared of any brush—as if someone made a habit of coming to an abandoned playground just to sit on a bench.

I wrapped my arms around my middle in a hug. A ridiculous laugh threatened to bubble up and out. This whole time, I was being led to a vine-infested swing-set, and a *bench*? My theory of hallucinations from my first day with the flu was fitting well with my new theory of pure insanity.

I was about to turn on my heel and find my way back home when I saw a figure among the trees in front of me. A chill skipped down my spine. I clamped my mouth shut and just stood there, staring. A pair of dark eyes stared back.

"What are *you* doing here?" The figure stepped out into the sunlight, revealing his identity: Jasper. His words held a level of disgust and anger that sent a stab of pain through me.

"Should I not be here?" I stepped back without meaning to, the coldness in his eyes sending my stomach into a fit of nausea. I took in a breath as he stepped closer, resentment radiating off of him strong enough for me stumble a little.

"Are you being serious?" he spat, making me want to crawl under something and hide. "Was the letter not enough for you? Now you have to torture me some more? Well, you can't. I'm done with your little games. This is *my* place, and you aren't welcome here anymore. You understand?"

I couldn't even open my mouth. Not only did I not know why he was so angry with me, I also didn't know why it was hurting me so much. I couldn't control the sudden tears swelling up in my eyes, and I struggled to keep them from spilling out.

"I—I'll just go," I mumbled after a few long seconds. At the sound of my voice a flash of something other than anger came into his eyes, but it was gone before I could decipher it. I stole one last look at Jasper before I turned and hurried back to the path, my heart racing unevenly.

My whole body was shaking. When I felt I was far enough away from the clearing—and Jasper—I leaned against a tree for support. I sucked in air and allowed the conversation to repeat over and over again inside my head until it started to make even less sense than before. Jasper had mentioned a letter...what letter? What happened between us to make him hate me so much?

I pushed away from the tree and stared down the path in the direction from where I had just come—toward Jasper. I was done being in the dark. I no longer cared if my memories dragged me back to my state of disobedience. They were mine, and I wanted them back. I *needed* them back.

~~~~~

The house was empty when I returned, and I felt like jumping into the air with joy. I had no desire to confront my family after my behavior in the kitchen. I didn't even know what I would say to them, especially since I had decided to keep my memories to myself.

I would have to face them eventually, but thankfully not right away.

Remembering that I needed to call Jenna, I grabbed the phone off the wall and locked myself in the safety of my room. I dialed Jenna's number, seven digits that I could never forget, and waited for someone to pick up.

"Hello?" answered a deep, masculine voice.

"Hello, Mr. Anderson, I was wondering if I could speak with Jenna? It's Luna." I waited as I heard him call Jenna to the phone. There was a shuffling noise as the phone was being transferred from one pair of hands to the next.

"Luna!" Jenna squealed. "How are you feeling? I heard that you had to cancel your OGS. That must be terrible." I had to stop myself from groaning. Why did everyone have to bring that up?

"I feel better," I said, completely ignoring her other comments. "I have kind of an odd question for you..." I could feel my heart speeding up as I prepared myself for any possible information she could have for me.

"Okay...let me hear it," she said slowly. I could almost see her biting her lip like she did when she was nervous.

"Did I ever hang out with a boy named Jasper during our senior year?" It was painfully silent on both ends.

"Jasper?" she repeated in a monotone voice. "I don't remember any Jaspers...oh wait, yes I do. That guy was a weirdo. You had to do a science project with him during first semester." Jenna rattled on, "I think I remember you hating him."

I felt deflated, disappointment churning inside me.

"Oh," I mumbled, my voice barely audible.

"Why do you ask?" Her voice held a faint urgency.

"I saw him on Oportet Day, and he acted like he knew me. He also seemed really upset, like I had done something to him." I withheld my other encounter with him. It felt wrong to keep information from Jenna, or from my parents, but in the name of self-preservation, it felt necessary.

"See. I told you he was a weirdo. Promise me you'll stay away from him, okay?" Jenna's voice seemed strained.

"I will," I lied.

Chapter Six

··

"There you are—I thought you wouldn't show," Jasper said as he looked up at me from a park bench. His eyes scanned the length of my body before he leaned back and stared up at the sky. "I'm guessing the only reason you did was for your grade's sake." He smirked in the most infuriating fashion. His jokes were becoming tiring.

I crossed my arms. "Whatever. Let's just get this over with." I couldn't help but stare at him as he gazed up at the dark clouds above us—the clouds that warned of a big storm's approach. "Maybe if we hurry we can beat the rain."

Instead of reading into my call to action, Jasper stayed leaning against the bench. "I've always loved how the world looks just before a storm. It's like everything is tinted a shade darker than normal." Jasper shifted his gaze back to me, as if searching my eyes for something. For what, I had no idea.

"You're delusional." I refused to give him the satisfaction of knowing that I agreed with him—that what he said reminded me of something I had always wished I could put into words. "Now come on, let's go."

He slid off the bench and moved to stand directly in front of me. "Do you like it here? In Oportet, I mean."

My entire body tensed. Was he crazy? What kind of question was that? Like the rest of Oportet, thoughts of what dwelled beyond our walls made me squirm. That was why I couldn't tell my parents that Jasper was my science partner—his family came from the Outside. A

41

portion of Oportet believed that our gates should close indefinitely—my parents included—while others believed it was our moral duty to recruit as many Outsiders into our society as possible. Because our leader, Tomlinson, believed the latter, anyone with prejudices against Outsiders had to keep those biases to themselves.

I shrugged. "Does it matter? Oportet is the right way—the right place—to live. Liking it is irrelevant." I thought I saw something like disappointment in his eyes.

I suddenly became aware of how close our faces were, and how just one step could close the distance between us. I looked away, to anywhere but Jasper. I felt a raindrop on my head and started walking toward Oportet's Museum of Science.

The museum was a large, modern-looking building with glass walls on the first floor. The glass next to the doors was plastered with colorful posters advertising different exhibits and special events. Jasper and I walked in a comfortable silence, like we could sense each other's minds deep in thought.

A group of children gathered just inside the building next to the bathrooms. They were all sitting, except one boy who appeared to be telling the others something very important. The boy waved his hands around as he spoke, and the other children listened attentively. The audience of other children appeared quite troubled.

I glanced at Jasper to see if he had noticed this peculiar scene, but he was staring off into space, still lost in his own thoughts. I had the sudden desire to know what he was thinking about, but this urge was blurred when I picked up on what the animate child was saying.

"I swear I'm not lying. It's the people here who are lying to everybody. It isn't really that bad on the outside—there are just some bad people. That's why my dad brought us here. He didn't want me to get hurt." The boy shrugged his shoulders. "I just wanna go back home though. I like it in California better than Oportet." The boy had bright red hair and freckles dotted his nose and cheeks.

"What's California like?" a girl asked, her eyes full of curiosity. The girl beside her scowled and crossed her arms.

A woman exited the bathroom behind where the red-haired boy stood, and a man who had been observing the children hurried over to her and angrily explained what they had been discussing.

"Christopher!" She bellowed, halting the boy mid-sentence. He whipped around, his entire face turning an unnatural shade of white.

Curious onlookers stopped in their tracks to absorb the unfolding conflict before them, and others quickly turned away to carry on with their business. I didn't have the strength to look away. I could feel Jasper beside me, but I couldn't peel my eyes away from Christopher's crippling fear and the woman's unflinching anger for even a second.

"Yes, Mrs. Tonya?" His voice shook slightly. The other children looked down at the ground or their laps.

"I thought I warned you what would happen if I caught you breaking another rule." She pulled out a paddle from her enormous purse and gestured for Christopher to stand up against the wall. She knelt down and repeatedly whipped the paddle across his rear with such force that his whole body trembled. Christopher had to be no older than nine years old.

After what seemed like forever, I couldn't watch anymore. I turned away, meeting Jasper's hardened eyes. I nodded my head towards the staircase, and we moved accordingly, haunted by Christopher's wailing echo against the silence of the first floor.

When we reached the second story, either the paddling had stopped or we were too far away to hear it. I breathed hard—and not from climbing the stairs.

Jasper remained silent as I pulled the research prompt from my backpack. I tried to swallow down my own feelings of discomfort. I suddenly wondered where Jasper was from, and if Christopher was telling the truth when he proclaimed that the Outside was better than what we had been led to believe.

Jasper's hand touched mine. My skin tingled from the electricity that jolted me from my thoughts. It lingered there for a few long seconds before he silently eased the prompt out of my hands to read over it.

Jasper broke the silence first. "You said that living by Oportet's standards is the right way to live. Why is it? What makes it the right way?"

I could only assume this outburst had to do with what we had just witnessed. I looked around to see if anyone was listening to us, but there was no one around.

"That—that was just screwed up," he said, then repeated, "Why are you so sure that this is the right way to live?"

I agreed with him that the paddling was a bit extreme for someone that young, but everyone knew Outsiders were forbidden to talk about their old lives before Oportet.

I cleared my throat, suddenly unsure of myself. "Because it just is. We have order and peace and—I don't know—protection, I guess. There is no fear of violence within our walls."

Jasper assessed my words and opened his mouth to speak, then closed it and handed me back the prompt. He seemed to be searching for the right way to get a point across. "I think that your council has put a lot of effort into convincing—no, brainwashing—this city into believing that life is only worth living if it is within their parameters. And the beating that poor kid just took looked pretty violent to me."

An uncomfortable silence hung between us. All I could do was stare at him with my mouth hanging open and my eyes too wide. Who the hell did Jasper think he was? If anyone had heard him say that, we would both be in a lot of trouble.

Jasper read my expression and shook his head like he regretted saying anything at all. "Sorry. Pretend I didn't say any of that. It was stupid of me." He let out a breath. "Let's just get this over with," he mumbled as he walked toward the physics exhibit, leaving me stiff and staring after him. He was wrong...wasn't he?

~~~~~

We spent all afternoon finishing the essay and the accompanying questions while listening to the loud thumping of rain against the roof above us. After the awkward situation from earlier, we didn't have much to talk about. Strangely enough, we returned to a comfortable silence, like the kind of silence between life-long friends. Or maybe it was that our thoughts were loud enough on their own.

I cursed my curiosity when I broke the quiet. "Where did you come from?" I blurted. The question had not come out exactly right, but Jasper seemed to understand perfectly.

His hand halted from where it was scribbling notes on a piece of lined paper, and he peered up at me with his head slightly cocked, his perfectly messy hair hanging down just above his eyes. "My mom and I lived near Oportet, in Portland.

"It was beautiful there. Most of the people who lived around us were friendly, and my mom—oops, I mean Mother—loved showing me the world. We did a lot of hiking and exploring..." Jasper shifted his eyes to behind me as he trailed off.

I thought that he must have been lost in his memories of Portland, but then I heard a deep voice erupt close to my ear.

"Well, what do we have here?" I spun my head around to meet the dark blue eyes of an unfamiliar face. The boy looked a bit older than Jasper and me, and I couldn't help but stare at his perfectly angular face, with a prominent jawbone and light brown, curly hair. I glanced nervously to Jasper. With all of their similarities, they had to have come from the same family.

"Luna, this is Alex...my cousin." And there it was.

I nodded—somehow losing the ability to speak. Alex radiated a kind of unsettling energy.

"Luna? That's a weird-ass name." Alex seemed far too amused by his breaking of a rule.

My immediate reaction was to scowl at his language. However, I bit back a smile as he made a show of looking around with eyes wide, as if he was making sure adults weren't around to chastise him. When he turned back to us and flashed me a mischievous grin, my composure broke, and I burst into laughter.

Did I really just laugh? Breaking a rule shouldn't be funny, right? But the more I thought about the guilt I was feeling, the more I started to question my guilt. What exactly was so bad about breaking this rule? Why did I keep having to suppress all of my thoughts that weren't up to par with what everyone kept telling me was right? Jasper's comment kept running through my mind: "I think that your council has put a lot of effort into convincing—no, brainwashing—this city that life is only worth living if it is within their parameters."

I wasn't brainwashed...was I?

"Well I'm glad you're not hanging out with one of those uptight girls, little cousin, or this would be awkward...." Then Alex winked at me.

Jasper was not amused. "What are you doing here?" he snapped. He seemed more than annoyed, tapping his pencil erratically on his notebook.

"I guess I was just thinking about where I could find a beautiful girl, and then I closed my eyes, clicked my heels together, concentrated really hard. When I reopened my eyes, I saw you," Alex answered, keeping his gaze on me.

I desperately hoped my face wasn't as red as it felt.

"Of course," Jasper said as he rolled his eyes. "I would expect nothing less."

Alex just smirked. "Give me a call if you ever need to discuss what a buzz-kill my little cousin is, Luna." He emphasized the word little, like he was trying his best to irritate Jasper. And with that, he turned and left, taking his air of arrogance and superiority with him.

"What in the world just happened?" I asked, my face still burning.

"Alex doing what he does best, of course." Jasper moved closer to me, his face inches from mine. "I need you to look into my eyes and listen very carefully, okay?"

I nodded, my eyebrows drawn together with curiosity.

"Stay far, far away from my cousin."

Chapter Seven

For a moment, I could not recall where I was or how I got there. I felt carpet beneath my body, and could vaguely remember entering the house after the walk in the forest, going up the stairs and into my bedroom. I talked to Jenna...and then I was seeing something from the past as I lay on my soft, carpeted floor.

I squeezed my eyes tight. I wanted more than anything to stay in the land of my memories. I willed the gears in my brain to turn and reveal more of what I had lost from the accident, but all I saw was darkness behind my eyelids. *Why did this happen to me? Why did I have to lose so much?*

My heart fluttered like a hummingbird, and my entire body was surging with excitement. I needed to see *more*. Now there were two people who I had encountered in my memories: Jasper and Alex. As I thought about Jasper's cocky cousin, I couldn't shake the nagging feeling that something unpleasant happened with Alex, and I was desperate to know what it was.

I knew that talking to Jasper about what I was remembering was not an option; he had made that quite clear. Every part of me protested against talking to my parents or Jenna...but what about Megan? My little sister seemed like the best option. Surely she knew *something* about Jasper and my past. The only thing that worried me was how to convince Megan to keep her mouth shut.

I couldn't help but feel like my parents and Jenna were hiding something, and Mother seemed bothered by the fact that I might regain my memories. I knew they all just feared that I would return to the me-of-last-year, but keeping any part of the truth from me was infuriating. It was hard enough that my brain had decided to completely erase an entire year's worth of memories, but for my own friends and family to lie to me about it?

I just hoped that somehow my instincts were wrong. Maybe the science project was the end of the interesting memories no one had told me about. That would mean that Jenna never lied to me about my relationship with Jasper, and Mother and Father told me everything I needed to know from last year.

I wanted to believe that my senior year was just as everyone had painted it: I defied authority, got into trouble, wanted to leave Oportet, had my accident, and then was granted a clean slate. I wanted to believe that my accident was the blessing that my parents claimed, but the thing about wanting things to stay the same was that life really didn't care what I wanted.

A voice in my head added: *The truth doesn't change just because you want it to.*

~~~~~

"Hey psycho," was the first thing Megan said to me when my family arrived home from the grocery store. I was making some soup in the microwave, prepared to eat in my room.

I glared at her. "Where are—"

"They're scared of you," she teased. When I shot her another look she continued. "They're still in the car...talking about your little freak-attack," Megan interrupted with a smirk. She was clearly enjoying this, and didn't care enough to hide it. "So um...what the hell happened?"

A part of me almost corrected her language, but then I realized that I honestly didn't care as much anymore. She seemed to think she was going to be chastised because her eyes widened for a split second, realizing she let a forbidden word slip in front of the Council's very own Golden Girl.

Her face relaxed when I didn't acknowledge her slip-up. Both of our heads turned as voices from outside gradually got louder and our parents approached the front door. I hurriedly grabbed the soup and a spoon, and gestured for Megan to follow me upstairs.

"Why?" She drew the word out in a long whine. "That's too far of a walk," she added, but I heard her footsteps behind me anyway.

"I need to talk to you for a minute," I answered. "By the way, you are probably the laziest person I know."

She giggled and closed the door when she entered my room.

"And you're the craziest person I know. Seriously, what happened in the kitchen? Mother was crying when you ran away. It was really scary. I've only seen her cry a few times..." She trailed off as she appeared to recollect the instances Mother has cried. They probably all had to do with me.

"I really need you to keep this a secret." I took a deep breath. "*Especially* from Mother and Father. If you can't promise to do that, then I can't tell you. Okay?" I studied her face as it moved from disbelief, to shock, to confusion, and then to curiosity.

"But that's breaking a rule...and I thought you didn't do that anymore." Her forehead creased as she tried to rationalize what was happening.

"Well, cursing is against the rules, too," I snapped. I knew that I should be more patient with her. After all, I'd given a speech against rule breaking at her school less than a week ago.

Megan looked at the ground, guilt written all over her face.

"I'm sorry. I didn't mean to sound harsh. That's not what I need to talk with you about." Well, it wasn't exactly harsh considering what her teachers or parents would have done if they had heard her instead of me.

"Okay, fine. I promise I'll keep your secret. This better be good." She offered a small smile, her eyes bright with anticipation.

"You know how my head injury took away some of my memories? And that the doctors said that there was no way I would ever regain them?"

Megan's face paled. Her eyes were wide and panicked, and the nervous habit of tapping her foot stopped.

"I don't think it's a good idea for us to talk about this," she finally said in a quiet voice.

"Why not?" *Why was this a touchy subject for everyone?*

"Because Councilman Tomlinson told me not to!" she squealed.

Now I was *extremely* confused. Tomlinson was the head of the Council, which meant he was also this town's leader. It would've been crazy go against anything he said.

"I don't understand...what in the world does Tomlinson have to do with this?" I couldn't understand how my amnesia was any of the Council's business. Why would they forbid my family from talking about it? Unless they were trying to cover up something...

My head was spinning. I knew *exactly* why Tomlinson would care. After my accident, I had been thrust into the spotlight, convinced of my fresh new start, and received the promise of a high-paying and well-respected job—all so I could build up the validity of Oportet's message. My captivating testimony of losing faith in the society and its rules, then rediscovering the gifts of protection and order that comes from within our gates was a hit. I was encouraged by the Council to give it to every form of media Oportet operates, to every school, and to every writer determined to publish the next Meaningful Novel. Tomlinson cares because whatever everyone is keeping from me is big enough to destroy his perfectly orchestrated show to his people, the show that reinforces society's faith in the rules and way of Oportet.

"Everyone needs to stop keeping things from me!" I exploded, startling Megan. She just stared at me with her big, green eyes. Her helpless expression made me feel sorry for her. It wasn't her fault, but I was far too angry to acknowledge that.

"I'm sorry, Luna," she whimpered quietly. "I wish that..." she trailed off, either struggling for the right words or holding back what she really wanted to say. "I'm gonna go." Megan gave me one last look of pity before she left the room.

I felt completely overwhelmed, and I was beyond irritated that I couldn't discover my lost memories all at once. I also couldn't control when they came, as shown by my near blackout in the middle of the day. All I knew was that I wasn't supposed to be getting my memories back at all, and that there was no way in hell I would tell anyone about this miracle. It was obvious that my remembrance would be considered a miracle only to me. I feared everyone else would consider it to be more like a curse.

My memories held the answers to my burning questions. There was no one to help me. I was on my own. Somehow, this did not scare me. The fact that my mind held all of the secrets and truth that the Council feared gave me a sense of power and determination. I just needed to remember that what I now felt could very well be stolen again.

I finished eating my soup. When I stood up from my desk chair to sneak my dishes down to the kitchen, I heard footsteps coming up the stairs and grow louder as they approached my room. I braced myself.

The person tentatively knocked on my door before walking in. I wished that it would be anyone but Mother. My hope collapsed as I took in the worried face framed by locks of bright red hair.

"Are you okay, sweetie? We're very worried about you."

I set my bowl on my desk and sat with her on my bed. I took a deep breath, feeling prepared after I had run through each and every scenario earlier that day. The concerned-mother-who-refuses-to-acknowledge-my-peculiar-behavior scenario was what I was hoping for. Mother had a fear of confrontation when dealing with something she found uncomfortable.

"Yes, I feel much better actually. I'm really sorry about breaking the plate and then running off like that. It was unacceptable. I just felt terrible this morning and wasn't thinking straight. When you reached for me, I was startled and my weak muscles just lost the grip. I was... embarrassed, so I panicked and ran." I took a breath. "I apologize for my behavior." I pushed my guilt-reflex aside as I managed to pull off my very convincing speech to Mother—who would have believed just about anything at that point if it meant we could forget that the incident ever happened.

"You're sure it wasn't anything else?"

I managed to keep my expression unchanged. Mother studied my face.

"What else could it have been?" I asked, lacing confusion through my voice.

"I don't know. I was just making sure you weren't hiding anything important from me. I appreciate the apology," she added, awkwardly patting me on the back. I forced a smile and yawn, trying to convey my exhaustion and desire for solitude.

Mother took the hint and left me to rest. I crawled under the covers, desperately wanting to disappear into the soft warmth and comfort of my bed. As I was drifting off, I heard yet another knock on the door.

I groaned. "Come in." My door was slowly and cautiously pushed open, as if I was a bomb and any sudden movements would cause an explosion.

"Luna?" Megan looked utterly frightened. That made me wonder what tactics were used by Tomlinson to instill such fear into my innocent little sister.

"Yes?" I tried to sound pleasant, but I really just wanted everyone to leave me alone and let me sleep. I was desperate for another memory.

"Father said to give this to you." She handed me a cream colored envelope with my name written in elegant letters. "Its probably just more fan mail."

"Right," I said, lacking the energy to carry on a conversation. I set the envelope on my desk and pulled the covers back over me.

When Megan disappeared out of my door, I grabbed the mail and tore into it. Inside was a small, square slip of paper with the same elegant handwriting. There were just three simple words written in bold, black ink.

Don't trust anyone.

Chapter Eight

··

I could not stop thinking about Jasper. His face, his smile, his voice...and most of all, I couldn't stop thinking about his bold way of voicing his opinions. How was it that he refused to fear his forbidden thoughts?

As children in Oportet, we were constantly warned of questioning the rules, the Council, or the ways of our society. What was there to question? The founders of our society were the only intelligent and rational individuals left after the fall of the American government, and when they established the rules, it was for a purpose. The core tenet of Oportet was that our lives matter. That was the whole and unadulterated truth. One of my childhood teachers expressed to the class: "The lives beyond our gates are nothing more than a waste of space. They are mindless zombies without a purpose, and without the truth that Oportet has discovered and given to its people."

I knew that Jasper must have been taught extensively about these views before his family was integrated into Oportet; this was a standard procedure for any incoming Outsiders. Once someone made the decision to become a citizen, they had to meet formally with a member of the Council. That councilman then referred the individual to a system of classes and workshops to instill in them each belief and value of our society. Why would you refuse to accept what the greatest intellectuals of Oportet had to say? There was no reason for anyone to lie in Oportet.

Yet, someone who heard all of our teachings—the teachings that made both logical and ethical sense—refused to accept them. I knew that I should stay away from this maddening and defiant boy, that I should have strong feelings of distrust or even hatred for him, but I could not will myself to feel anything more than exhilaration. I knew it was wrong, but I wanted to talk with Jasper about his views. I wanted to discuss all of the thoughts and questions I had suppressed for years. Scariest of all, I wanted to know him.

We managed to finish our project all in one day. I wished that we hadn't, so that I would have an excuse to see him again. A part of me also longed to see Alex again—partly because of Jasper's strange warning against it. It was interesting to be around someone who radiated rebellion and confidence so strongly. It was everything I was supposed to loathe.

I had never experienced the feeling of being drawn to the wrong people, the people who were destined to cause all kinds of trouble. I'd been cautioned about rebels by countless authority figures, yet it was somehow easy to dismiss their warnings once I was actually feeling this pull. I felt drawn to Jasper in an unexplainable way—a way that demanded to be acted upon.

I was trying my best to concentrate on my math homework, but I was distracted by everything. I groaned and laid my head down on my notebook, unable to continue.

I heard the faint ringing of the phone from the other side of the house, and I willed it to be Jenna, calling to rescue me from my hellish calculus worksheet.

When I heard footsteps getting closer to my room, my mood instantly lifted.

Father pushed open my door, holding the phone with a peculiar expression on his face. I smiled and reached for it, my excitement causing Father to look at me rather suspiciously. Was he wondering about the status of my homework? He obviously wasn't too worried if he was giving me the phone; Jenna and I were known for our marathon phone conversations.

I held the phone to my ear and waited for Father to go. He looked reluctant to leave. I lay back on my bed and held the phone to my ear.

"Hello?" I expected to hear the usual loudness of Jenna's many siblings in the background, but the other line was eerily silent.

"Hey Luna." I shot up into a sitting position. My heart sped up to a frightening pace, and I had the honest fear that it was going to explode in my chest.

"Jasper," I breathed. I was at a loss for words. Calling me was at the bottom of my list of things I expected from him. We had finished our project, so why had he called?

I heard him chuckle to himself on the other end. "You seem surprised. You don't have a line of suitors keeping you up at night with their constant phone calls?" Since he couldn't see my eyes roll through the phone, I tried my best to send it telepathically. Who used the word suitors anymore?

"Sorry. They usually call in the afternoon."

"Oh really?" Jasper asked, clearly amused. A long moment of silence followed. "What are you doing right now?"

I laughed. I was unaccustomed to talking with anyone other than Jenna on the phone.

"Procrastinating, as usual."

"What class?" Jasper seemed at ease, like calling someone he barely knew was completely normal for him.

"Calculus." Then, to my astonishment, Jasper began to hum. I strained to hear the quiet but distinct melody. It was beautiful, soft and sweet.

Jasper suddenly became quiet. "Oh, sorry. I forgot that music was a touchy subject for, um, the people here." Music, like any other potential *form of spontaneity, was only permitted through appointed musicians whose work had to be approved by the Council. "Doesn't it bother you that you aren't allowed to be creative?" Jasper asked like questioning the foundation of my values was the same as asking about my favorite color.*

I opened my mouth to say something like: "No, creativity leads to rebellion, and rebellion will leave you no better than those from the Outside. If everyone were allowed to be creative through writing, music, film and art, then chaos would ensue. Oportet would fall just like the government of our past nation," Instead, I just shook my head. Those words were not mine. They were etched into my brain in a way I had never given much thought to. It was a page in a textbook. It was the voice of my teachers and parents.

"Yes. I hate it." I blurted the words before I could stop myself. They became an engorged river whose dam had just collapsed. I could not control them as they rushed out, a frightening jumble of thoughts that had always been suppressed. "I hate that I can't write stories that aren't true, or write about how I really feel. And I don't just hate that I can't write how I feel, I hate how I can't even say or think how I feel!

"I hate that I am told to believe that our founders were somehow the most intelligent people ever to have lived—that somehow they were able to receive the truth of how we should live our lives, and then offer no explanation to how they could possibly know that what they say is the actual truth." I paused to take a breath, too caught up in my ranting to realize the magnitude of what I was saying to this near-stranger.

The words I had just uttered slammed me hard in the chest. That was not how I was supposed to think. That was not how I was supposed to act.

"Wow," was all Jasper said. "That was unexpected."

"I'm so sorry. That was uncalled for...I can't believe I just said any of that. Please don't tell anyone." My body was shaking. I had never expressed anything of that nature to anyone—not even Jenna. I just felt like I could with him.

"It's fine, seriously. Of course I won't tell anyone...besides, who would I tell? It's not like the kind people of Oportet are jumping to be friends with the new kid from the Outside."

I let out a breath of relief as he rushed to reassure me. "Thanks," I said softly, feeling vulnerable and embarrassed for my outburst. I didn't even know if I meant any of that.

"I actually like you a lot more now."

I bit my lip, ashamed of everything I had just said despite Jasper's compliment.

"I have no idea why I called you. Sometimes I just do things without really knowing why. I've learned that generally, I have good instincts."

"And what are your instincts telling you now?" I held my breath waiting for him to reply.

"I'm going to wait and see if they're correct before I tell you."

There was that infuriating humor I had come to know. "What was that song you were humming earlier?" I could barely remember what it sounded like, I just knew that is was the most delicate and lovely song I had ever heard.

"Oh, um, I think it was Clair De Lune by Debussy. My mom loves classical music, we were playing it earlier..."

I couldn't believe he had just admitted to me that he snuck illegal materials into Oportet. How could someone trust so blindly? The whole conversation we were having seemed surreal.

"Yeah, let's keep that a secret too, okay?" Jasper laughed, like he had just admitted to eating the last piece of cake.

"Sure." I was beginning to feel a strange sort of happy, like I was free to say anything I wanted, without any guilt or repercussions. I felt strangely comfortable.

"Clair De Lune is French for moonlight. You know what Luna means, right?" Jasper asked.

I thought back to any conversations with my parents about my unusual name. Then I remembered Aunt May telling me that she had chosen the name, but she had never specified why, or what Luna meant.

"No."

"Huh," Jasper said. "Well, Luna means moon. In ancient Rome, it was the name given to the Goddess personifying the moon. I can't believe your parents—from what I've heard, they're quite extreme—would allow that kind of name to be given to their child. It's very different. I've found that people don't like different around here."

That was startlingly accurate, especially the part about my parents.

"How did you know what my name meant without even looking it up? Do you just store random, irrelevant facts in your head?"

Jasper laughed. His laugh was the kind of laugh that was contagious; you just couldn't help but feel happy, too.

"Don't worry, my knowledge doesn't extend to practical affairs, so I wouldn't be able to help you with that calculus homework. I just read a lot of books."

I wondered if he had a stash of illegal books in addition to the music.

"Well, I used to read anyway. The books here are way too boring for me."

I let my curiosity get the best of me. "Do you have books from the Outside?"

Jasper paused, speaking slowly when he decided to trust me with more information. "Yeah, we do. We just brought the necessities." He laughed quietly to himself, like I'd missed out on a private joke.

"Why are you telling me this?"

He was silent for a moment, like he was wondering the same thing. "I trust you."

I didn't know how to respond to that. The entire phone conversation seemed like an odd dream. "So let me get this straight. You decided to call this girl on a whim who you had only spent time with once for a school project, and then spill your family's secrets, even though it could land your entire family back behind Oportet's walls." It defied logic. "I don't understand."

Not to mention, Jasper had already admitted to knowing my family's conservative Oportet values. He must have also heard about how much my family hated Outsiders...

"You're right; I'm crazy." That was a step in the right direction. "How about we change the number of times we've hung out outside of school? I could show you all of the terribly wrong things we brought from the evil Outside, if you wanted." Now we were back to being insane. "Oh, and if we are pinning the tail on the crazy here, let us not forget a certain someone screaming all kinds of terrible things about her self-proclaimed Utopia."

That was true, but the sting still made me want to hit him through the phone. I felt my cheeks growing hot as I thought about my embarrassing outburst.

"Please promise to forget about that. That's not how I really feel..." I was struggling to find the right explanation for my behavior. Maybe it was how I really felt, but I hated myself for the confession. Who knew how Jasper would hold it over my head?

"The truth doesn't change just because you want it to. Stop beating yourself up for admitting that you can see through the cracks in this flawed system."

I was both irritated by and in awe of his words. How did someone so young learn how to speak like that? Or have the confidence to speak like that?

"By the way...you never answered me. Do you want to hang out sometime?"

"I was hoping you were just joking about that," I said, laughing nervously. I didn't think I could handle confronting Jasper face-to-face after this—after I had just bashed what I had stood for my entire life.

Instead of being offended, Jasper remained his usual amused self. "I was actually expecting a much worse response than that. What do I have to do to get you to meet me at my house tomorrow?" What? His house? "Some consider me quite charming. I've never had to work this hard before."

I snickered. "Oh I'm sure."

There was a knock on my door, making my heart skip several beats. What if someone heard Jasper and me talking? What if they heard what I said about Oportet?

"Hold on a second, Jasper," I said in almost a whisper. I set the phone down on my desk in a hurry.

"Luna?" Mother said as she pushed open the door. "It's getting late, I think you should get to bed soon." I nodded. Things had been awkward between us since she struck me last week for cursing. "Your father told me that your science partner called earlier...what was his name, again?"

I thought quickly. Father must have asked for a name when Jasper called, and Jasper must have been smart enough to give just a first name. My parents would have recognized his last name in a heartbeat.

They were very involved in Oportet's government, and new Outsiders were a very big deal to the Council. The Council held new residents in the same shroud of suspicion as residents showing rebellious tendencies, which were considered strictly detrimental to our society's well being.

Hopefully they hadn't already singled out Jasper.

"Oh, that was Jasper. He had a question about the project we did Saturday." I tried to sound disinterested.

"You never told us that your project at the museum was a partnered project."

I put on my best look of innocence.

"I'm sorry—I didn't think it mattered. I'll be sure to let you know in the future."

Mother pursed her lips. She hesitated a moment, tapping her fingers on my desk. "Your Father and I need to know who you are with at all times, is that understood?" I nodded once more. "Goodnight, Luna."

"Goodnight." When she left, I grabbed the phone off my desk and flipped off the light switch. My room instantly became pitch black, and I struggled for a moment to find my way to the bed.

"Are you still there?"

"Yep."

"I think your insanity has officially rubbed off on me."

"Why is that?"

"Because I'm going to come over tomorrow. And you can show me all of your music and books—and whatever else you brought from Portland."

"I knew my charm would eventually win you over. It always does."

I smiled into the darkness. I was thinking strange and exciting new thoughts—thoughts that I had never allowed myself to dwell on before.

"We can't tell anyone about this. My parents would rip out my lungs if they found out I was sneaking off to your house."

Jasper laughed at my choice of fate. "Feuding families and sneaking around—classic Romeo and Juliet scenario."

"Who are Romeo and Juliet?" I assumed he was referring to something forbidden from Oportet.

"Wow. You kids really are deprived of great literature. It's considered a classic back in the real world. My grandma had me read it a few years ago. She started ranting about how my mom wasn't giving me a proper education, and that her English professors made her read all kinds of boring shit to make her more intelligent.

"She was the one who got me into reading. It was better than sitting around waiting for the next big catastrophe to happen. People on the Outside may be free, but your parents aren't lying when they say it's dangerous out there." Jasper was very quiet on the other line, and I could sense something very troubling in his voice.

"Dangerous?" I thought this whole time Jasper had been hinting that the Outside was better than Oportet. "I want you to tell me all about it...when we're sneaking around and such." I was grinning, expecting Jasper to laugh. He didn't.

"I'd rather not."

Suddenly everything was serious, and I had an indescribable feeling of unease in my stomach. It felt like I had somehow dug up something Jasper needed to keep buried.

"What's your address?" I asked, quickly changing the subject. I used the small lamp on my bedside table for light as I dug around in my backpack for a pen and paper.

"Do you have something to write it on?" Jasper sounded distant.

I grabbed my calculus notebook and pencil after flipping my lamp back on. "Yeah. I'm ready."

Chapter Nine

I woke up in a deep depression. I didn't want to eat, I didn't want to move, I didn't want to communicate with anyone, and I didn't want to continue living my life like everything was okay. Nothing was normal anymore. I just wanted to *remember*.

I spent five days trying to access more of my memories. I felt like screaming and crying like I did as a child when I didn't get my way. I spent my time going through the motions, attending whatever event the Council invited me to, and giving more testimonies, speeches and interviews.

Eventually I decided that forcing the memories to surface wasn't going to work. I just had to be patient and let them come on their own, but patience wasn't exactly a trait I had been blessed with. It was going to take a lot of work.

~~~~~

"Luna, we're worried about you," said a faraway voice. "After you hurt your head, and after all of those counseling sessions—you were happy. You were back to normal: motivated and ambitious. We've noticed you seeming... off, lately. It's concerning."

Father cleared his throat. "Yes, your mother is right. This was how it started last time. You were fine one minute, then the next you completely ignored everything you had ever been taught. You had no interest in all of the things you used to adore."

I fought the urge to glare at my clueless parents. They had no idea what it was like to feel completely in the dark. It was one thing to know that everyone was hiding something from me, but I couldn't even remember my own past. "I'm not sure what you're talking about. I've been involved in all of the things you and the Council recommended, and I have been preparing for my OGS for a while now." I kept my voice calm and steady as I watched my parents exchange unconvinced looks.

"Are you sure that nothing is on your mind? Anything you need to talk to us about?" Father asked, searching my eyes for evidence that I was hiding something.

"No, really, everything is fine. I've just been caught up in my work. Choosing the right job is stressful." The three of us were sitting at the kitchen table. Megan was at a friend's house for the night. I had barely touched my soup, and figured that I should probably start gulping it down if I wanted to do a better job at seeming normal.

"And how is that going? Have you narrowed down your choices?"

I had faked a list of occupations that I knew would please them. Planning my future seemed pointless without my past. It was becoming an unhealthy obsession.

"Yes. I want to either hold a position within the government, or become some sort of teacher or school counselor." My parents seemed satisfied with my answer—much more so than when I blurted out my love for writing. That was a lost cause.

"Those sound like respectable jobs, and I could see you excelling at any one of them. I am excited to see what Councilman Tomlinson has to say when he advises you tomorrow," Father said.

I almost choked on the soup in my mouth. "How do you know that he's the one who will be meeting with me?" The head councilman rarely used his time to host an OGS. It was usually one of the newer councilmen, or even an adviser like Father.

My parents must have misread my surprise, because they smiled at each other and then at me like it was the best day of our lives.

"He called us personally. He said that he couldn't wait to help you advance on your career path. He has some high expectations of you. I hope you can live up to them." Mother's grin grew wider. I tried to smile back, but I feared it looked more like a grimace.

"That's a lot of pressure," I muttered.

Father was quick to give me a pat on the back. "You can do it, sweetie. You've been preparing for this your whole life. It's time to finally become an adult."

I didn't think I could handle being an adult if it meant I had to bow down to a man who forced my family to lie to me.

~~~~~

I thought about the anonymous note I'd received earlier in the week: *don't trust anyone*. I wondered if Jasper had sent it. Thinking about him made my stomach feel all kinds of crazy. Well, thinking about the past version of Jasper did. I wasn't sure the current Jasper would be too enthusiastic about helping me. But who else would have sent the note?

I paced back and forth in my room, dreading the Occupational Guidance Session. One-on-one interviews and meetings with adults were always the bane of my existence. Such interactions made me so anxious that my entire body shook. My voice faltered, and I often forgot most of what I'd planned to say.

I sat down on the carpeted floor of my bedroom and tried to calm myself down. I started to act instinctively, like when I somehow knew the way to the abandoned playground in the middle of the forest.

I sat with my legs crossed and took deep breaths. I visualized each of my worries being sorted out into categories in my mind, and then sectioned them into padlocked crates.

I kept taking long and soothing breaths as I cleared my mind. I acknowledged any thought that presented itself— careful not to *consciously* create any thoughts—then let it pass on its own. Jasper popped into my head on more than one occasion.

A burst of noise jerked me from my relaxing trance.

"Luna? Are you ready to go?"

"Yes," I said, a bit irritated. I was much calmer after employing whatever technique I'd just pulled out of my mind. I hoped it was something else that would reveal itself in my awakened memories.

When I snuck a glance at my clock, I saw that twenty minutes had passed. I shook my head in disbelief. That didn't seem possible.

The meeting was being held in one of the middle school's conference rooms, so I could easily walk there from my house. I endured all of my family's fussing and advice giving before I headed out, my relaxed state quickly dissipating.

I smoothed down my elegant black dress and ran a hand through my freshly curled hair. I looked pretty today, maybe even beautiful.

Mother had made sure I looked my best for this meeting. I felt odd walking on the side of the road in a formal dress, heels, and my dark red lipstick.

When I crossed the busy road that separated rows of houses from the school building, I noticed a familiar car in the parking lot. There was a woman in the passenger seat staring at me, prompting me to look down as I passed her.

I heard the slamming of a car door behind me. "Luna?" A feminine voice asked cautiously.

I turned around and assessed the woman, trying my best to associate her with any names or events. It was to no avail.

"I'm sorry, do I know you?"

She looked at me like I had just asked her to undress. "Look, I know that things ended badly between you two, although he avoids the subject whenever possible, but I don't understand why you are acting so childish about it," she chastised. "I thought you were better than that. I *know* you are better than that." She just shook her head at me like a mother who had just caught her child in the act of committing a misdemeanor.

Could she be Jasper's mother? Was Jasper the person things had ended badly with?

The woman had long dark hair that she had pulled back with a flowery headband, and kind green eyes. She looked like the kind of person who you could share anything with, the kind of person who would comfort you when you hit rock bottom. Maybe that was who she had been to me, but there was no way for me to know that without any recollection of it.

"I honestly don't remember you, I apologize. Last spring I—"

"You'd better go." The woman was looking over my shoulder anxiously. I turned around to take in the trouble approaching. *Jasper.*

"What the hell?" I heard Jasper mutter in the distance.

I left the perplexed woman and hastily made my way toward the building. I didn't have the strength to face the confusing version of Jasper making his way towards me.

Instead of letting me pass, Jasper jumped into my path. I stopped and stared into his dark, haunted eyes. Time froze as we faced each other, our bodies only a foot apart. I tried to breathe normally as he scanned the length of my body before his gaze stopped at my lips. He looked away.

"Luna," he said, sounding exhausted. It was the first time he had said something to me without any resentment in his voice. "Why are you doing this?"

"I honestly don't know what I'm doing."

Jasper ran his hand through his hair, looking away from me with obvious frustration.

"I don't know because until last week, I didn't even know your name."

Jasper snapped his head back to me. "What are you talking about?"

"We knew each other last year, didn't we?" I was unsure of myself, what if my memories weren't memories at all? What if they were simply dreams with only a small part of the truth?

Jasper stared at me incredulously. "Are you being serious, or are you still screwing with me?" His eyes narrowed as he tried to understand my words.

"Last year I tripped on the steps of my front porch and hit my head. I fractured my skull...how did you not know about this? Your Mother seemed to think we were close." I tossed a glance back to the woman standing outside her car.

Jasper just stared at me.

"Was this before or after the letter?"

I remembered him mentioning this letter to me in the forest. "I don't know anything about a letter. I've been remembering some things lately, but I've had to keep it a secret because I'm not supposed to be remembering." I paused. "I suspect that my fall was no accident."

Jasper was staring off into space. He was wearing dark jeans and a nice button-up shirt. He had probably just come from an OGS.

"So the letter came before," he murmured. He cast a nervous glance back at the school building and then at me. "I'm sorry, I can't do this right now. I don't know what to believe—"

"Stop acting like the victim here!" I interrupted. "You have no idea what it's like to lose an entire year's worth of time, and then realize everyone is lying to you. You never know who you can trust, and you constantly feel all of these emotions without your mind providing any explanation for them."

"Luna, you have no idea what you did to me last spring. I'm sorry about what happened but I have to go." The notebook he was holding slipped from his hands and landed between us. He looked at me strangely and nodded his head toward the ground. I squinted at him in confusion before I understood.

I bent down to pick it up at the same time Jasper did. He snatched it from the ground and leaned closer to me.

"Don't tell him anything," he whispered. "If someone caused your accident, it was him. I'll find you later so that we can finish talking." Jasper pulled himself up and walked toward the car that his mother was leaning against. It was obvious that she'd been watching us the whole time.

I watched as she got into the passenger's seat, letting Jasper slide behind the wheel and speed away.

I turned toward the building and saw Tomlinson staring at me from the glass doors. That explained Jasper's words and behavior. I wondered if Tomlinson had counseled Jasper as well.

Everything felt better after talking to Jasper. It felt so natural, so right. He said that he was going to find me later. I was finally going to sort everything out, and get the answers I so desperately needed.

"Was that boy bothering you?" Tomlinson asked as the door clicked shut behind me.

"No, he was just confused. He thought he knew me but he must have been mistaking me with someone else." I gave him a sweet smile. Tomlinson looked old and tired, his face withered and hair thinned.

"Ah," he said, content with my faked ignorance.

He led me to one of the conference rooms, the locks of the door clicking into place when it closed behind us. I sat down with my pen and notes, trying not to shake like I usually did when I grew anxious.

"Let us begin." Tomlinson looked at me almost pityingly, which only fueled my anger towards him. *I was more aware than he thought.* "You will be earning substantially more income in whatever occupation you choose because of your helpful service to Oportet." I nodded. "What line of work did you have in mind?"

I was trying my best not to reach over the table and slap the smug little smile right off his face. I knew in my heart that he was behind it all—Jasper had just confirmed what I had felt all along. As if any amount of money would ever cover the costs of what he did to me. Was that how he got rid of opposition? Did he stage an accident just because I wanted to leave Oportet last year?

We went over the jobs I had picked out, discussing what my best fit would be based on my interests and talents. Tomlinson was very insistent that I consider working in the government like my parents, which made me set on choosing one of my other two options.

Tomlinson stressed in detail how much training and higher education was needed for each job, and I took notes accordingly. I tried to concentrate, but my thoughts enjoyed distracting me, and I had a hard time telling them to stop.

The most devious thought of them all was of Jasper. I ran his words through my head, both in my memories and just moments ago. I needed to talk to him soon.

In the middle of writing a word something strange started to happen. I was seeing two different things: my pencil hovering above the paper and a white, wooden door with a house number on the top. I tried to snap out of it—now was not the time to relive one of my memories. I was in the middle of an Occupational Guidance Session with Oportet's leader, of all things. I felt myself slipping....

No, no, no. Focus.

My head was spinning and starting to throb. I noticed Tomlinson squinting at me, and I realized that I was staring at him. His mouth was moving but I couldn't hear any of his words over the unbearable ringing in my ears.

Deep breaths. I was struggling to hold on to reality—the *current* reality, not the past. I was reaching my hand out to knock on the door, but was also massaging my temples at the same time. This needed to stop.

"I'm really sorry, Mr. Tomlinson... I'm getting a migraine." I could barely hear myself talk. My voice seemed far away.

I focused in on Tomlinson's moving mouth and was able to hold my memory at bay. I just hoped I hadn't lost it for good.

"That's all right, you are free to go. This session was almost over anyway. Just remember to contact the Occupational Placement Office when you make your decision." I managed a weak smile and shook his outstretched hand.

~~~~~

It was Saturday, so everyone was either at one of Megan's soccer games or at home. I thought I remembered Mother mentioning a game today.

I burst through the front door to a quiet home. No one was rushing to bug me about my OGS, so I assumed they were all out of the house.

My memory was still alive and insistent, urgently asserting itself into my mind's forefront.

I lay back on my bed, staring up at my ceiling. In seconds I was transported to a different time and place.

Chapter Ten

....

My knuckles rapped on Jasper's door three times. We barely talked at school today, but I caught him staring at me more than once. I couldn't say that he was the only guilty one, either.

So this was it. I was officially lying to my parents and going to an Outsider's home. There had to be something wrong with me.

The door opened, and to my surprise it was Alex who was smirking on the other side.

"You again, huh?" He stepped to the side to let me enter the small two-story home. "So did you live in Oregon, too? No, wait, Washington. You look like a Washington girl."

"No, I've always lived in Oportet," I replied.

Alex stared at me in bewilderment. "That was a joke, right?" He was smiling expectantly, like I was about to give him the punch line.

I shook my head.

"And I was just starting to like you." Alex cast a glance behind me and leaned forward, his mouth right next to my ear. "I think I'd like you anyway." He slowly retracted, waving at something behind me.

I turned around to see Jasper raising his eyebrows at us from what appeared to be the kitchen. He narrowed his eyes at Alex, who backed away with his hands raised in front of him, much like Megan did in her soccer games when she was trying to let the referee know she didn't commit a foul.

I turned to glare at Alex, who was obviously using me in whatever feud he was in with his cousin. Alex winked at me like he had in the museum. I rolled my eyes.

"Hey," I said when I reached Jasper. He led me past the bright-colored kitchen and into a room with blue walls, a couch and a TV.

"How are you?" Jasper asked politely. He knelt down on the ground, rifling through a bin filled with CDs in labeled sleeves.

"I'm fine. I've just never done this kind of thing before." Oops, that came out wrong. "I mean, do something that my parents would hate me for." Even worse. What was going on with my ability to speak coherently? English was beginning to feel like a second language.

Jasper looked up at me, his eyes tinted with concern.

"Your parents would never hate you. They might be pissed at you though...Listen, we don't have to do this. I don't want to get you in trouble." He studied my face. "Or make you feel bad."

I shook my head. "They just have a thing against Outsiders, which is ignorant considering everyone originated from the Outside in some way or another."

Jasper nodded, still appearing skeptical.

"And I wouldn't have come if I didn't want to."

Jasper seemed to weigh my word choice as he finally found the desired CD. "Ah, here it is. I promised you some illegal stuff, didn't I?"

I stared at the disk labeled Nirvana. I'd never heard that word before, and I wondered if it had a meaning or if it was just a made-up word.

"I have no idea what your music taste is, since you've never heard any before. I'll just play things from different genres, and you can tell me what you like or dislike."

"I've heard music," I protested. There were a few instrumental albums I used to study, composed by the appointed musicians of Oportet.

Jasper grinned and shook his head at me. "I meant real music, Luna."

I loved it when he said my name—the way it rolled off of his tongue like it was his favorite word to say.

Jasper stuck the CD into a laptop and waited for it to load. The sudden burst of noise that shot out when he clicked the little triangle button made me jump. Jasper laughed, crushing my hope that he hadn't noticed.

"Sorry about that. The volume was up all the way," he said as he turned it down.

We sat on his couch in silence for the duration of the first song, Jasper casting amused glances my way every few seconds. I was swept away by the singer's smooth, captivating voice as it transformed into angst-filled aggression. I had never heard anything like it before, and I wasn't sure I was enjoying it.

"It's one of the oldest albums we have," Jasper murmured. "What do you think?" He looked at my face, appearing to be holding back laughter.

"I don't know. Could we try something, um, softer, maybe?" I hoped that all of the music from the Outside wasn't as rough.

Jasper finally let out the pent-up laughter, whatever he thought was so funny apparently had to do with me. It made me so angry and nervous all at once. Was it something I said?

"I was kind of just messing with you. I just wanted to see how you would react. Nirvana isn't exactly what a native Oportet citizen should be starting out with."

I let out a breath. I was glad all his music wasn't like that. I shot him a mock look of irritation.

"Definitely not what I'm used to." I watched as he pulled out an album by Coldplay.

"Now tell me what you think of this." Jasper replaced the Nirvana CD with the new one, and once again pressed play.

I was in awe. It was so much better than anything the musicians of Oportet could create. Everything about it was perfect. It made me want to burst into tears. Music had never made me feel that way before.

"I love it."

"I thought you would. It's those spot-on instincts again."

I smiled as he played each of his favorite songs for me, all by different artists and with different styles. So many of them spoke of love. Was that how I was beginning to feel about Jasper? Did I want him to be more than just a friend to me? I had never felt that way about anyone before. Even when I had a crush on someone in middle school, or when I thought I liked one of the boys I hung out with in high school, my feelings had never seemed so real—so exhilarating. How could I feel that way about someone I barely knew?

All at once I became aware of how close our bodies were, separated by his laptop. I looked at him, and he met my gaze. For a moment we just stayed that way, taking each other in. Was he thinking any of the things I was, or was something terribly wrong with me?

A petite woman wearing a white blouse and a long green skirt appeared in the doorway. She had wavy, dark brown hair like Jasper's, and bright green eyes that radiated joy.

Jasper gestured to me. "This is Luna. Luna, this is my mom."

I had to get used to the slang he brought from the Outside. In Oportet, children had always been instructed to refer to their parents as Mother and Father. I didn't understand why it was so improper to use other names. I supposed it was just another way to alienate anyone from the Outside.

"Hello, dear," she said with a smile.

I stood up and shook her hand like I had always been taught. I hoped that this wasn't another thing unique to Oportet.

"Nice to meet you." I smiled back at her. Music was still playing in the background, and I wondered why she wasn't freaking out because of whom her son was letting listen to it. I could get them into a lot of trouble. It could even resort to their immediate expulsion from Oportet.

"Luna...what a pretty name," she said. "Oh, and you can just call me Lilly." My first thought was how lilies were my favorite flower, and how much the name fit this petite, delicate woman. She transferred her gaze to Jasper and said, "I need to go grocery shopping. Do you need anything?"

"No, I think I'm good." I looked between Jasper and his mother in disbelief. Was she really leaving us alone? My parents would have cut their eyes out before leaving one of their daughters at home alone with a boy.

"Jeez. Your moth—mom—is very trusting."

Jasper shrugged. "Yeah, she has trouble with knowing how to be a parent. She was far too young when she found out she was pregnant with me. It took her by surprise, to say the least," Jasper stated, like it was a simple fact of life.

I wasn't sure how to respond. "Oh," I managed.

"Now imagine how she must feel having to take in my delinquent cousin."

"What is going on between you two? Do you just not get along?"

Jasper laughed without humor. "Some people are just...bad. You can argue whether it was nature or nurture that made him that way, but the fact still remains: Alex is not a good person."

"What do you mean?" He might have been flirtatious, or even arrogant, but I didn't see how this could be enough to classify him as a bad person.

"My cousin is a sociopath. He isn't capable of real emotions."

My eyes widened. Now that was a valid reason to distrust his cousin.

I was about to say "Oh" again, but I decided that once was enough. Instead, I settled on "I'm sorry." I meant it, too. It must have been hard to live with someone with that kind of mental disorder.

"I want to show you something," he said, shutting the laptop. He was obviously finished talking about Alex.

He navigated through the rooms of the house until we reached the back door. He pulled it open and let me pass through, all gentleman-like. I would have appreciated the gesture more if his mischievous smile wasn't making me so nervous.

"Where are we going?" I asked. "How do I know that you're not the sociopath leading me to my death?"

Jasper jerked his head around and looked at me with one eyebrow pulled up. I tilted my head back with laughter.

"Life is all about chances. Not taking them doesn't make you smart—it makes you weak." Jasper said. "That's the real secret for how to live."

I considered his words. Was that really the secret? Were the people of Oportet weak because they avoided taking risks?

"Who's to say what's the right way to live?" I thought aloud. "Everyone knows the exact same amount of nothing when it comes to understanding our purpose in the world." I spoke quietly, like my parents were going to suddenly jump out from the shrubbery and lock me up somewhere.

Jasper looked at me—he really looked at me—like he was trying to see into the depths of my mind. If he found anything, I hoped he'd let me know, because I wasn't even sure I understood the jumbled mess I'd become.

"*Are you sure you spent your whole life here?*" *Jasper finally said as he led me into Oportet's forest.*

"*I was just wondering that same thing.*" I let out nervous laughter, surprised by what I was revealing to this boy yet again. "*It's like I'm finally allowing myself to think about things without anyone else's influence.*" I felt like I was jumping into this abyss—a huge black hole that might lead me to a terrible demise...

Or land me exactly where I needed to be.

"*That's exactly what the people here fear. But free-thinking gives you power.*" Jasper held a tree branch back for me to pass through. For some reason, my usual discomfort among the tall, dark trees and gnarled branches was held at bay. I felt safe with Jasper.

"*Please tell me where we're going,*" I begged as we headed further into the woods. I hated when I wasn't aware of everything happening around me.

"*Someone needs to work on her patience skills,*" Jasper teased, finally coming to a stop.

"*You need to have something in order to work on it,*" I muttered. I tried to see what was ahead of us, but Jasper was blocking me.

"*Close your eyes.*"

I blinked at him. I crossed my arms in defiance and waited for him to let up and let me pass.

"*Come on, take a chance.*"

I rolled my eyes at his playful grin, which never failed to pull a smile out of me. "*Fine.*" I closed my eyes and waited. I felt his hand close around mine, causing my heart to miss a few beats.

"*Okay, now move forward.*" I cautiously took a few steps, opening my eyes a little to make sure I wasn't going to trip. "*Hey, no cheating,*" Jasper snapped. I closed my eyes all the way again, irritated that I had been caught.

I was walking at the pace of a dying snail. As I let myself pick up speed I felt my foot collide with something on the ground, and my already terrible balance was completely lost. I gasped as I felt myself falling, Jasper's hand slipping through my fingers.

My eyes flew open in a panic, but instead of hitting the ground, I was suspended above it. I felt hands on my waist, keeping me from plunging into the forest floor. Jasper pulled me up, and I was thankful to be back on my own two feet unscathed.

"God, Luna. It's just walking. It's really not that difficult." His hands loosened from my waist, cutting off the electrical impulses his touch created.

"You're the one who was supposed to be guiding me, asshole," I said as I elbowed him in the stomach. He clutched the spot I hit and doubled over dramatically.

He straightened up, throwing me a taunting grin.

"We need to work on your elbowing skills, too, maybe after we work on your patience?" That was easy for him to say. It felt like elbowing a brick wall. "Turn around," Jasper instructed.

I narrowed in on him. "I'm not sure I can trust you anymore." Now it was Jasper's turn to roll his eyes.

"Don't be difficult."

I turned around, not quite sure what to expect. I saw some sort of swing set beyond the group of bushes in front of us. Where were we?

I pushed through the vegetation, entering what appeared to be an ancient playground in the middle of the clearing. There were three swings hanging on the swing set and two slides—one large and one small for different ages of children. There was also some kind of metal spider web, which was now a rusted brown color.

Even stranger was a single wooden bench in the middle of it all, perfectly preserved, with no signs of rotting or withering.

I felt Jasper behind me, and I couldn't help thinking about the way his hands felt on my waist. He was making me think crazy things, utterly insane things. I wanted to collapse into his arms; I wanted to know him: his fears, his regrets, his passions, and his secrets— everything.

"Cool, right?" Jasper asked as he moved to stand in front of me. "I stumbled upon it when I was out here exploring."

"Why are you showing me this?" *Why was any of this happening?* "I mean, why me?"

Jasper nodded as he understood what I was trying to say. Did I even know what I was trying to say?

"You remember what I said about chances? The principle applies to people, too." Jasper reached his hand up to my face, catching a stray lock of hair and placing it behind my ear. "I brought you because I think you're pretty great."

Chapter Eleven

....

I struggled as the scene faded out, wishing for more time with these particular memories.

Jasper and I had talked for hours as we lay on the forest floor, meeting in our special little place time and time again. A month's worth of time was being thrown at me in a matter of seconds.

Then, it was all over.

I was trying so hard to pull my past from my stubborn subconscious that I gave myself a headache. I didn't want to be living in the present anymore. I needed to be with Jasper in the past.

I wondered when "present" Jasper was going to make an appearance. I needed to explain everything to him and for him to fill in the gaps. Most of all, I needed to know why he had been acting so resentful towards me. I couldn't imagine why I would ever hurt someone like Jasper.

~~~~~

"Tell us all about it," Mother said, nearly shaking with excitement. Megan was eyeing me from her seat at the table.

I proceeded to tell my family about the meeting, leaving out the part where I had to flee the scene, my memories attacking me. My parents looked proud of me as I spoke. Megan just looked anxious, exactly like she had ever since I tried to question her the week prior.

"Were you expecting a call from anyone today, Luna?" Father asked, taking a huge drink of his water.

"No, why?"

Father's eyes narrowed slightly, setting his fork down. "It was actually quite strange," he said. "I heard the phone ringing, but when I answered it, the person on the other line hung up."

I immediately thought of Jasper. He promised to meet me later so that we could finish talking without tipping off Tomlinson.

"That is strange," Mother murmured.

"Oh, and we ran into Jenna while we were out," Father said. "She seemed hurt that you hadn't been making any effort to see her lately. Did something happen between you two?" Jenna had told me that we had grown apart before the accident, my memory-wipe bringing us back together. I didn't think I could fully trust her until I knew what had torn us apart last year.

I was about to reassure my parents about our relationship, but Father cut in. "I told her that she was welcome to come over tonight at six so that you two could catch up."

I managed a smile, but that was *not* on my list of activities for the evening.

"Is that alright?" he asked, which seemed like a silly question; it wasn't like we could call and disinvite her.

"Yeah. Sounds good." It was hard enough acting normal in front of my family, but acting like I wasn't having a mental crisis in front of my childhood friend sounded like a miserable chore. She knew me better than anyone, and I couldn't help but remember what she'd told me about Jasper. She told me that I hated him, and then she made me promise to stay away from him. This made me even more suspicious of her. It seemed like everyone was trying hard to keep me away from Jasper, and from anything that could trigger a relapse of my old self.

After dinner, I waited in the family room listening to one of the only music albums we owned. It was dull and *safe*. It was like the musician was scared of composing a melody that evoked any kind of emotion. I yearned for Jasper's music, so full of passion and fire.

The ring of the doorbell brought me off the couch and to the front door. I let a smiling Jenna into our foyer, and we snuck off to my room in silence.

"We've had such good times in here, haven't we?" Jenna sighed. She was examining my room, as if she was looking for any major changes.

"Yep. Have you had your OGS yet?"

Jenna nodded. "I've decided to be a pediatrician," she announced. "What about you?"

"I'm not one-hundred percent sure...but I think I'm going to become a teacher. A high school English teacher would be my first choice." It was the closest I could get to what I really wanted—to write. I didn't know what I wanted to write about, exactly, but I knew that it would never be a viable option for my future.

"I think you'd be good at that." Jenna grinned. "So..." She hesitated for a moment. "Jasper hasn't bothered you since we talked last, right?" At the sound of his name, my heart sped up.

"Who?" I faked confusion, surprised at how easy it was becoming to lie and play dumb for people. At least I was lying for self-preservation. No one else had a valid excuse. "Oh, sorry, you mean that boy I was asking about earlier. Haven't seen him since," I said.

"That's good. I was worried about you. We wouldn't want Oportet's rising star to be attacked by some street freak." Jenna laughed. "I'm just really glad you had your little accident. It gave me my best friend back."

I stared at her in disbelief. "Did you really just say that?" I spat.

Jenna shut her mouth, her eyes widening. "I'm sorry, I didn't mean that I was glad you got hurt or anything... but I mean, it's not like you haven't said those exact words to me before. Just a month ago you were telling me how thankful you were that you had this fresh new start." Jenna wrung her hands. "It sucked that it took you cracking your head open to finally realize the error of your ways, but *you* were the one who said that you were glad it happened."

I was fuming, not just because of what I was hearing come out of Jenna's mouth, but also because it was true. I *had* said those things, and I had believed them.

"You're right. I did say that, but that was before I started to realize that I only knew a fraction of the truth. That was before I knew that people were using my memory loss for their own benefit." Anger boiled inside of me, lacing my every word with venom.

"No, Luna. We have all been using your memory loss for *your* benefit. The sooner you realize that, the sooner everyone can finally move past this." Jenna's eyes were fiery as she spoke. "How do you think I felt watching you completely shut everyone out, completely disregard everything that you have ever stood for, and completely turn away from Oportet?" Was that moisture forming in her eyes? "It felt awful, Luna."

I watched as raw emotion grew in her eyes, and I lost track of my anger for a moment. I was going to say something about how not having any recollection of last year was awful, and that she couldn't possibly compare her pain to mine, but weren't we both hurting?

I knew that Jenna was wrong, and I knew that she was misguided in her attempts to protect me, but I also knew that it wasn't her fault. We were all raised the same in Oportet. There just came a time when we each had to choose whether we would listen to what we were told, *or to ourselves*. Everything I was remembering was pointing to the fact that I had chosen the latter. That was exactly what everyone was so afraid might happen again.

"I think you should go," I said.

Jenna didn't protest; she wanted to leave just as much as I wanted her gone. Her long, jet-black hair fell from behind her ears to shield her face.

"I really do want the best for you," she said quietly. "I know that things aren't perfect in Oportet, but it's much better than what you would get Outside." She gave me a pointed look.

I nodded without agreement. I was beginning to doubt that, possibly for the *second* time in my life.

~~~~~

It was a few hours after Jenna left when I heard the phone sound in the distance. I sped down the hallway and pulled it off the wall before the rest of my family heard the second ring.

"Hello?" I asked, letting out a breath when I heard the familiar voice on the other end.

"Luna," Jasper said. "Meet me in the clearing as soon as you can, okay?"

"Okay."

~~~~~

Jasper was waiting for me when I made it to the foliage-covered playground. The sun was almost down, and the beautiful colors of the sunset were just starting to fade into pale pastels.

Jasper was lying on his back, his eyes on the sky. When he heard me approach, he pulled himself up, giving me an expression I didn't recognize. I walked hesitantly to him and sat across from him in the grass, pulling my knees to my chest.

"Tell me everything," was all he said.

So I did. I told him all I knew about my head injury, the timespan that I was told I had lost forever, and the memories that I was slowly regaining. I watched the different emotions flicker across his features: surprise to pain to confusion and back again.

"All of what you told me is either extremely suspicious or completely impossible," Jasper said when I was finished. "Actually, it sounds both."

"I know."

"So you just randomly start having visions whenever and wherever, and you've been getting them all in chronological order? That's just insane."

When I had finally said it aloud, it really did sound like a beautifully intricate lie.

"It's killing me because I just want to see everything at once, but I have to wait hours or even days between memories. I'm very impatient."

"I know you are," Jasper murmured. "You haven't even remembered the best things yet."

"Like what?"

He smiled. "No, I shouldn't ruin the story for you. The plot needs to develop before you get to the good stuff."

I glared at him. Only Jasper could pull off a joke about something this serious. "This isn't funny, Jasper." I crossed my arms.

"No, it's not." His smile faded. "But it could be dangerous for you to remember too much too fast. Maybe it's best to let these memories come back to you slowly. It would probably be a lot to process all at once. I mean, it sounds like you suffered quite the head injury."

I thought about his words. "You're probably right." I sighed.

"Well, this really is a turn of events isn't it? It makes me wonder..." Jasper trailed off, caught up in his thoughts.

"Wonder what?"

"Nothing. The sooner you remember everything, the better."

I remembered what his mother, Lilly, had said about our relationship having a bad ending. It made me sad when I thought about what had possibly happened between us for Jasper to act so spiteful. "Why did you hate me before I told you all of this?" I asked.

Jasper looked up at me, his eyebrows drawn together. "It's not possible for me to hate you. I was just hurt."

I looked down at the ground, careful not to meet Jasper's pained eyes. "Why?"

"I know it's selfish, but I would rather not get into that now. This is the first time I've really talked to you in months."

I sighed, but was grateful that we could skip the seriousness for once.

"As much as I've tried to deny it, the truth is that I've missed you," he said.

"I think I've missed you too." That was a lie. I *knew* that I had missed Jasper. I knew that I had missed him since the very first memory.

"So, um, am I stuck in the friend zone?" Jasper fiddled with pieces of grass, looking up at me and flashing me his trademark look of mischief. "I assume that it's only common courtesy to wait until you remember all of the romantic stuff before I can make a move." Jasper grinned and I froze, snapping my head up to look at him.

"So we were..." I had no idea how to finish that sentence.

"Together?" Jasper nodded. "That's how the trouble always starts, isn't it? Boy meets girl, boy and girl are not supposed to be together, and then they decide to be together anyway."

"Like *Romeo and Juliet*," I whispered, remembering Jasper referencing to the piece of literature in my memories.

"What was that?" Jasper asked, looking at me curiously.

"Nothing." Desire was flooding through me. Of course we were together. It was how it was meant to be. Everything I had been feeling for him since I started getting my memories back pointed to this truth. I wasn't feeling drawn to him because I needed answers. I was drawn to him because I needed *him*.

When I awoke in a hospital bed with no recollection of anything past junior year, I knew that something other than my memories was missing. Something powerful was taken from me, something that left me crying and laughing and screaming and fighting, and feeling *alive*.

I didn't know how much I'd sleepwalked through life until Jasper opened my eyes. He woke me up. I didn't need a memory to tell me what I already knew: I never stopped loving Jasper, even when I couldn't remember his name.

I didn't care about common courtesy; I just wanted Jasper to close the gap between us. I had no problem with a *second* first kiss if that was what it took.

"Come here, Luna," Jasper said, like he wanted to get rid of the space as much as I did. He was looking at me so intensely that I wanted with all my heart to remember every word, every touch, and every bit of his heart that he had ever revealed to me.

I sat up onto my knees, my face inches from his. We were completely motionless for the longest time, like we were both wondering if this was the best idea, but it was far too late to decide against it.

I was already reaching my arms around his neck, and he had his hands on the sides of my face, holding it there in front of his. Jasper leaned in, pressing his lips to mine.

My first thought was how much the sensation made my body feel like it was on fire. Why didn't the flames hurt me? Could Jasper see them? They were engulfing every part of me.

I pressed into Jasper, our lips completely in sync—like the act was the most natural thing in the world—like we had kissed a thousand times before. For all I knew, we had.

For the first time in weeks, my mind was completely quiet. Everything was at a standstill. It even seemed plausible that the Earth had stopped rotating around the sun, giving Jasper and me this moment all to ourselves. I thought that the world owed it to us; we had both lost so much.

We were gasping for breath when we finally pulled apart. I was in complete bliss until I saw the look in Jasper's eyes.

"What's wrong?" I asked. How could *anything* be wrong? Hadn't my memories been trying to tell me just how right this was?

Jasper took his hands off my face and pulled himself up, letting my arms drop back to my sides. He offered a hand to help me up, but I managed without it, irritated at him for ruining the moment.

"I need to take you home." Jasper was running a hand through his dark hair, his eyes hardened and cold. "That shouldn't have happened."

"I don't understand," I said. Jasper was walking so quickly that I had to run just so I could place myself in front of him. He tried to dodge me, but I moved with him, blocking him until he talked to me. "Isn't this what you wanted?"

Jasper muttered something under his breath before meeting my eyes.

"I don't want to be with you like this. It's not right. You're just going to remember why you wrote that letter, and this is all going to be over."

I let Jasper push past me. The only light was coming from the moon above us, and I struggled to watch where I was going.

"Please explain the letter to me," I begged. I assumed it was what I gave Jasper to end things between us. I needed to know exactly what I wrote.

"You told me how you really felt. You thought you were in love, but you really just wanted to rebel...against your parents or the Council...I don't know. You said you weren't going to leave with me because you realized it was a mistake." So I didn't just want to leave Oportet—I wanted to leave with Jasper.

"That's ridiculous! That doesn't even make any sense," I said.

"That was my first thought too, but even if all that was completely made up, you still made it very clear that you didn't want to be with me anymore. You said that you were done making a point and just wanted to go back to the way things were before—before you met me."

I shook my head. I would have thought those things in my memories if they were true.

"I didn't write that letter. I know I didn't." I saw something dart across the ground in front of me and suppressed a girlish squeal. The huge coastal trees were looking more ominous than they had before.

"And how do you know that? You aren't even close to remembering whether or not you wrote the damn thing."

I recoiled against the harshness in his voice. "I just know, okay? I know because what I've been feeling for you both in the past and in the present is the most real thing I've ever felt." Jasper kept moving forward, but he slowed his pace to a normal walking speed.

We were both silent as Jasper led me back to my house. I was glad he seemed to know where we were going because the trees, rocks, and fallen branches all looked the same to me.

We were standing in front of my house now, completely bathed in darkness. I was looking down at my feet, not able to look Jasper in the eyes. How could he think so little of me? I would never hurt him like that, and I would never make up such silly excuses.

"Let me know when you realize how much of an asshole you're being," I said. I didn't wait for his reaction before storming away.

I slipped through the front door, careful not to make too much noise as I eased it shut behind me. I leaned my back against the wood, letting myself slip down to a sitting position. I buried my head between my knees, but miraculously suppressed all tears attempting to surface.

The house was dark, but I could see a streak of light coming from Megan's bedroom. I hoped that no one had noticed my absence, or I would have to explain myself tomorrow.

I didn't want to move. I wanted to sink into the floor. What if I did write that letter? What if I had a good reason to end things with Jasper, and I made up those excuses because I *wanted* to hurt him? I knew exactly how to cause him pain, and I could have taken advantage of that knowledge.

No. That was impossible. The sooner I remembered the real story, the sooner I could fix my relationship with Jasper. I just hoped that it was still recoverable.

Chapter Twelve

I was happy. Things that normally paralyzed me with dread didn't seem that bad anymore. School was the prime example of this—I could get through the day because I knew that Jasper would walk me home after school, like he had for the past two weeks.

"I don't like this," Jenna said when she caught me smiling at Jasper from across the math classroom.

"Like what?" I knew exactly what she didn't like.

"Whatever's happening between you and the Outsider." Disgust coated her words. What had gotten into her? This wasn't how best friends were supposed to act.

"He has a name," I snapped.

"I don't care."

I shot her a glare.

"You don't think he actually cares about you, do you?" Jenna shook her head, her apathetic smile raising the hairs on the back of my neck. She looked at Jasper, who was looking adorable concentrating on his math problems, with a kind of coldness in her eyes I had never seen before.

"What is your problem? You do realize that your grandparents came from the terrible Outside don't you? We're all Outsiders," I retorted, getting Jenna to shut her mouth for the rest of class.

"Don't come running to me when you get hurt," Jenna said as the dismissal bell rang.

"I won't." I watched as she strutted out of the classroom, whispering something to Cassie James like a pissed-off ten year-old. Cassie cast a glance in my direction, and then turned back to Jenna.

Jenna had been acting distant ever since I swore her to secrecy about hanging out with Jasper, but this was a low blow. We had both despised Cassie James since the day freshman year when she told everyone I threw myself at boys for attention. She caught her boyfriend coming on to me and assumed it was a mutual attraction. It wasn't.

Jasper was waiting for me when I came out of the classroom, but I wasn't really in the mood to talk. His smile faded as he scanned my face.

"Hey, what's wrong?" he asked.

I hated myself for letting my eyes tear up, as they did whenever I was extremely angry.

Jasper wiped away the single tear that escaped with his thumb, looking at me with worry etched in his eyes. "Your eyes get bluer when you cry. They look really bright."

I smiled weakly. I took deep breaths, needing to get air into my lungs in order to calm myself down.

"Luna, talk to me. What's going on?"

I explained the situation the best I could, knowing that most of it would be over his head considering he didn't speak teenage-girl.

"That's really petty," Jasper said when I was done.

"I know. I just don't understand why she's acting like this." We stepped inside the science classroom, taking our seats that were across from each other at the lab table.

"You're changing, and that's scaring her." The rest of the class was shuffling to their seats as we spoke. I was glad that Jenna had English this block.

"I don't feel like I'm changing; I feel like I'm becoming more myself."

Mrs. Lawrence made her way to the front of the classroom, surprisingly quick with a bulging stomach that looked like it would break her back if it grew any more. I was half-expecting her to go into labor in the middle of class. I had heard that today was the last day she would be teaching as she prepared for the arrival of her twins.

"Do you want to take a detour on the way home?" Jasper whispered after Mrs. Lawrence turned her back to draw a diagram on the whiteboard.

"Sounds good to me," I whispered back. I could faintly hear Jasper humming something, using his pencil as a drumstick on his notebook.

It was causing me physical pain to hold my laughter back, and it was getting harder and harder to suppress my amusement as I watched Jasper switch to jamming on an invisible guitar. I looked around to see if anyone else was seeing the show, but we were in the back of the classroom so I had the performance all to myself.

"You are such a freak," I whispered with a smile. He ignored me, taking the nonexistent instrument and slamming it on the table for his finale.

Jasper looked up at me and grinned. I shook my head at him.

"Just admit it. You think me and my air guitar are hot."

I narrowed my eyes. "I will admit no such thing."

The rest of class was incredibly dull as we worked in our textbooks in silence. It was too quiet for us to even whisper. I was tapping my foot absentmindedly as I watched the clock count down the seconds. The bell rang, signaling the end of the school day.

"Well, that was excruciating," Jasper said as we packed up our things. We handed our work to Mrs. Lawrence on our way out, rushing out one of the school's side doors before the parking lot was flooded with moving cars.

Both the high school and the middle school were in close proximity to my neighborhood, so it wasn't a long walk home at the end of the day. Oportet was beautiful today, the brightly pigmented leaves just starting to break free from the trees. Autumn was the rest of my family's favorite season. I was the only one who preferred winter.

Jasper respected my wish to leave my parents in the dark about our friendship, or relationship, or whatever it was. I knew that they would throw a tantrum, or worse, forbid me from seeing him. They would watch my every move, which would prove to be detrimental to the times I snuck out to meet him at our spot in the forest under the guise that I was going for a walk or to the library.

We walked in a comfortable silence, admiring the changing autumn scenery. My life was starting to feel like a dream—more fantasy than reality. If someone had told me a few months ago that I would be falling for someone like Jasper Williams, deliberately breaking rules, sneaking behind my parents' backs, and saying out loud what I had been suppressing my entire life, I probably would have dropped dead from a heart attack.

"I'm ready for summer," Jasper announced as we entered our secret space.

I raised a brow. "We haven't even been on fall break yet. How could you be thinking about summer?"

"Haven't you noticed?" Jasper faced me, his head cocked to the side, an amused smile growing on his lips.

"Noticed what?"

He strode over to the swings, tipping two over to let the debris and fallen leaves spill off. "Time is moving a lot quicker than it used to, Luna."

I sat down next to Jasper, twisting my swing so that I faced him.

"I think that it should be addressed as a global issue—just below climate change."

I smirked. "You are the most...interesting person I know." I lowered my voice to a mock whisper. "Interesting is code for crazy by the way."

"So far today I have been called crazy and a freak. Feel free to add to the list."

I laughed at Jasper's hurt expression, quickly replaced with an indignant grin.

"And just so you know, you suck at insults."

"Maybe that's because I wasn't really trying to insult you. Maybe I like that you're a crazy freak." As soon as the sentence was out I felt heat flood my cheeks. Did I really just say that?

"Luna Beckham, are you flirting with me?" Jasper teased. I hoped that my face wasn't as red as it felt. I had never been as good at flirting as Jenna.

I immediately shut out the thoughts of who I thought was my best friend. If she wanted to act so immature and ignorant, then she'd better do it far from me.

I opened my mouth to give Jasper a clever retort, but I stopped when I saw his expression. The air was heavy, the intensity high enough to feel. Surges of energy swirled around us.

Jasper was leaning in, my mind debating whether to run or to meet him halfway. I wasn't sure if I would ever be able to breathe again, or if my heartbeat would ever regulate itself.

It was too late to run as Jasper finally kissed me. My eyes widened, not sure how to react to his lips on mine. It was sweet and gentle, and not at all what I expected. I shut my eyes and gave into my instincts.

The awkwardness dissipated as we found the perfect ways our lips could meld. I had never thought you could feel two polar opposites at the same time, but vulnerability and safety coursed through me as we connected. I felt a piece of myself break free, transferring to Jasper. I knew I was giving him the power to rip that piece apart—into a million different particles—leaving it so destroyed that I would be missing that part of me for the rest of my life. I no longer had complete control of my heart.

But I trusted him. I had to trust him. He wasn't like anyone I'd ever met. He was breathtakingly honest and raw, unapologetically opinionated but respectful, and he liked me for me. The whole me, not just the obedient me, the me who let everyone but herself rule her life. He saw me for what I was, not for who I pretended to be.

Jasper was the first to pull apart, and much needed air filled my lungs. He searched my eyes, and I shook my head at him.

"What is it?" Jasper asked. Panic flashed in his eyes, and he slowly lowered the hands that had been cradling the sides of my face.

I smiled. "Took you long enough."

~~~~~

I did not want to go home, so I went somewhere I hadn't gone in years—Aunt May's house. My parents convinced us that Aunt May was a bad influence around the time I began middle school. It was unclear why they had decided to draw a line between us and Aunt May, but I couldn't help but wonder if it had something to do with the rule she broke for me—the rule against storytelling.

I took my parents words against my loving aunt to heart, and tried my best to clear my feelings of unease. I figured that it was better for me to stay protected from my aunt's wrong ways than to question my parents' judgment.

But I was questioning everything now.

I slowly raised my hand to the doorbell, took a deep breath, and pressed it. I tapped my fingers against my thigh, catching myself humming one of Jasper's favorite songs.

I was on the verge of concluding that the house was empty when I heard footsteps on the other side of the door. May swung the door open, a look of surprise forming when she saw me.

May was much younger than Mother, with curly blonde hair and beautiful features. When I was young, I dreamed of being the flower girl at her wedding, but the years went by and Aunt May miraculously remained single.

"Luna?" Aunt May stared at me skeptically, cocking her head to the side. After a few long seconds she shook her head and put on a smile. "Come in, dear."

I entered her quaint home, noticing the changes that had taken place since my last visit. Everything was so clean and orderly, perfect for having company over, but I couldn't imagine Aunt May having many friends in Oportet.

"How are you?" she asked, leading me into the kitchen.

"I'm..." I was a lot of things at that moment. "Changing," I blurted.

May pursed her lips, gesturing for me to take a seat in one of the barstools as she put a pot of water on the stove.

"Peach tea?" She offered, as if I hadn't said a word.

I was flooded with memories at the sound of my favorite childhood beverage. Flashes of a younger me running around my beautiful aunt's home. And memories of my fingers curled around a warm mug of tea, talking for hours with my favorite (and only) aunt.

I was built for colder weather, the heat of summer keeping me hidden indoors. At the end of a day with my aunt, I'd collapsed on the couch. I'd listened to her intricate stories as she made them up on the spot, my eyes fluttering as I'd tried to stay awake to hear the endings.

Thick socks kept my feet warm on a cold winter day, my eager eyes would take in May's lovely curls, bouncing as we danced, the smell of hot chocolate and pine trees in the air. Aunt May would read from a forbidden storybook about a mysterious day called Christmas. I'd listened with excitement and wonder as she described a magical man who flew around the earth, giving presents to every child as they slept.

"Why doesn't Santa visit Oportet?" I always asked, feeling disappointment and dread envelop my innocent heart.

Aunt May then explained that Santa Claus had retired; his late night travels were too dangerous for him in his old age.

I learned the truth when I was older. Christmas was strictly forbidden from Oportet. In a moment of childlike disobedience, I had decided to go against Aunt May's warning for me to keep her stories between the two of us. Before I could even finish my retelling of "The Night Before Christmas," I was torn away from my classmates and given a severe paddling. I lied and told my teacher that I had overheard older kids in my neighborhoods telling the story. My teacher figured they were disobedient teenagers from the Outside.

Now at my aunt's house for the first time in way too long, I realized that I had been staring off into space. I had so many memories with my aunt, yet I hadn't spoken to her in years.

May raised an eyebrow.

"Sorry, um, tea sounds good," I mumbled.

"So...changing," May murmured, reminding me what I had said when I entered.

"Why did you break rules with me?" I asked.

May dropped the teakettle, and it clanked loudly as it slammed down on the countertop. Her eyes widened as she fumbled for the teapot and placed it on the burner.

"I didn't think they were right. You were just a child...." She looked away. The marble counter was suddenly more interesting than looking directly at me.

"How did you even get that stuff from the Outside?" At this, her head snapped up, finally meeting my eyes. I remembered a hidden stash in her pantry where she kept a collection of storybooks, novels, and music. I never told anyone, even when I learned how wrong she was for having the forbidden media.

"Why did you come here, Luna?" She asked, avoiding my question. Her tone was soft, curious even, like she was urging me to tell her everything.

I took in a breath. "I have questions...about Oportet. And I needed to talk to someone. Someone who understands."

May pressed her lips together in a thin line. She fidgeted with her hands as the kettle began to wail. She poured our tea in silence, leaving me doubting my judgment. May was younger when she was breaking rules for me...what if she had changed? What if she was going to get me in trouble with my parents, or worse, the Council?

"You haven't spoken to your parents about this, have you?" She tapped her fingers on the counter as she waited for my answer.

"No." How could I? They would freak out, maybe even force me to meet with some kind of counselor for troubled teens. Questioning the mechanics of Oportet was never taken lightly.

Children can get away with asking the why questions, but the answers were to be where the discussion ended. There was no place for dwelling upon any perceived flaws in the system, because everyone was taught from a young age that the system was perfect. The Council was perfect, the rules were perfect, Oportet was perfect—and if I were to believe that all of those things were true—then I was perfect.

"Well, don't," May said. "They're too far gone to be rational, but you've obviously woken up. You have a chance now, Luna."

"A chance for what?"

May smiled. It was a smile full of sadness and pain, yet it was also filled with something else—hope.

"A chance to be free."

Chapter Thirteen

....

ittersweet. Seeing Aunt May alive was as depressing as it was joyous. As the happiness of having a conversation with May surfaced, the reality that I would never be able to talk to my beautiful aunt again darkened my memories. She was gone, and nothing from the past was going to change that fact.

I lifted a hand to my mouth, as if the sensation of Jasper's lips on mine could have left a tangible mark. I liked the kiss from last night much better than the kiss from my memory. It was obvious that we had improved over time. Not that it mattered, considering the shredded state of our relationship. Maybe all I had were my memories.

Morning light streamed in through my open window, and a breeze swept through my room, blowing papers off my desk and tickling my bare skin. I pushed out of bed and slammed the window shut, catching a glimpse of a note on the floor in front of me. I picked it up, immediately recognizing the handwriting from the last note warning me not to trust anyone.

This one read: *No one can know you remember.*

The only person who knew I was remembering things was Jasper, but he already knew I was going to keep this a secret. Why was he being so paranoid? Plus, I thought he was angry with me. Not that this bipolar behavior was any different than his actions these last few weeks.

One day I was a three-headed monster with fangs, the next Jasper kissed me like I was the air he needed to breathe. Now he was freaking out about a letter I may or may not have written. The back and forth was giving me whiplash.

I made myself promise to push all thoughts of Jasper out of my mind, as hard as that would be. I'd made it clear last night that I wasn't coming to him. If he wanted to see me, he'd have to make the effort.

I needed to figure out what happened to me last spring without tipping off my family or Councilman Tomlinson. I was growing certain that my accident was a case of foul play, a powerful reason to stay quiet. If Tomlinson found a way to take away my memories once, then he could do it again. Whatever screw-up that allowed me to remember might not happen a second time. The thought of losing Jasper—of losing *myself*—forever sent a stab of pain through my chest. I would fade into the mindless robotics of Oportet, and I doubted I could find a way to wake myself up again. Tomlinson would surely know better the second time around. I'd never be left alone. I'd be constantly monitored. I was not going to let any of that happen.

I would not forget again.

~~~~~

I was bored out of my mind by the end of the week. I hadn't recalled a single memory since Saturday, and I was stuck when it came to investigating my accident. Who was I even supposed to talk to about it? The only people with the answers were the ones who couldn't know I was on to anything. I couldn't help but think of how Jasper would know what to do.

Not thinking of Jasper was impossible. The fact that he hadn't made an effort to see me made it even worse. Why did everything have to be so difficult with him? It was easy to be with him in my memories but I couldn't pinpoint what had changed.

Of course I couldn't. I hadn't remembered it yet. That realization painfully illuminated my need to remember. The frustration of not being in control of my own mind overwhelmed me. I was being suffocated.

It was Friday night, which meant Megan was off at a friend's house. Lately she seemed to be at her friends' houses more than her own.

Both of my parents were home from work, but they barely acknowledged my existence during the past week. I usually got some sort of "what have you been up to today?" from Father, and a "have you made your decision yet?" from Mother. They wanted me to make up my mind about my occupation.

I slowed just before reaching the living room, the sound of hushed voices lashing out at each other from the kitchen freezing me in my tracks. I crept up to the closed door, struggling to make out my parents muffled words.

"He got the note! I left it on his porch and then watched him pick it up and bring it into his house." Father sounded exasperated, and I couldn't make out Mother's reply. Her voice was much lower in volume. "He should feel nothing for her now," Father said insistently.

Mother said something else, still too low for me to hear.

"Fine. I'll talk to her." There was silence for a moment. "You know it doesn't matter anyway. She doesn't remember him."

My heart beat wildly inside my chest, the realization of what my parents were discussing hit me hard. I was certain it wasn't me who wrote the letter last spring, but I had no idea why my parents would have.

I scurried away, settling on the couch with my book about teaching high school English. I already knew my choice, but telling my parents would mean that my future in Oportet was locked into place. I wasn't sure that was what I wanted anymore.

"Luna? Where are you?" Father called.

"Living room," I replied, on high alert after what I had just overheard. Footsteps approached, and I was careful not to lift my head from my book. I scanned over the words without actually reading them.

"I need to talk to you about something." I lifted my eyes as Father dropped down on the couch across from me. "Why are you reading in the dark?" he asked before I could say anything. I looked around, for the first time noticing the lack of light.

"Oh, um, I don't know," I mumbled. He raised his eyebrows at me before flipping on the lamp.

"Are you familiar with the name Jasper Williams?" I struggled to maintain my composure at his bluntness, but then I remembered that no one knew about my regained memories. That name should trigger no emotion from the memory-wiped Luna.

I appeared to be thinking hard. "I...I don't think so." I paused. "Wait, maybe. I think Jenna told me that he was the creep who keeps talking to me. I think he's crazy." I watched Father's face visibly relax.

I took a deep breath, my palms sweating. I subtly wiped them on my floral skirt, hoping he wouldn't notice.

Father cleared his throat. "Yes, well, this young man is not someone to associate with. Let me know if he tries to talk to you again, and we can do something to tip the scales of his trial."

"Trial?" Unease rushed through my veins. Something was very, very wrong.

Father took in a breath, obviously debating on whether or not to reveal any more on the subject. After a brief pause, he continued. "The Council has reason to believe that Jasper sympathizes with the Outside."

What did that even mean? Was this my fault?

"We're fairly certain how the Council will rule. Don't you worry, Luna. You know what happens to disorderly Outsiders." My head pounded, and I stopped breathing altogether. Jasper might be kicked out of Oportet.

"They'll kick him out," I deadpanned, slowly letting out the breath I held. I sensed a hint of worry leaking into my voice, and Father's eyes flickered to me.

He looked away before speaking. "Yes," he said finally, in almost a whisper.

~~~~~

I had to call Jasper. He needed to know that I didn't write that letter, that I remembered our real first kiss, that I was beginning to remember being in love with him, and that he couldn't go. I wouldn't *let* him go.

I leaned against my bedframe, listening to the phone ring in my ear, holding onto it so tight that my knuckles ached.

"Hello?" Lilly's sweet voice sounded on the other line. I detected a hint of nervousness in her voice. Was she afraid that it was the Council calling? Was she afraid that they were going to take her son away?

"It's Luna. Can I talk to him? Please?" I bit my lip, feeling more and more dread with each passing second that the other line was silent. She had to let me talk to him.

"You remember."

I let out a sigh of relief. She didn't hang up. "Yes, I remember."

"Jasper told me about what happened. He never tells me anything anymore...." She trailed off.

I didn't have time to discuss the dynamics of Lilly's mother-son relationship. "Can I please talk to him? It's important." I no longer cared how impatient I sounded.

"Yeah he's right—" I heard shuffling, and an exchange of words between two voices. I assumed one was Jasper; I was so close to hearing his voice. "Oh, um, I'm sorry. Jasper isn't here anymore."

"What do you mean he's not there anymore?" I wanted to bang my head against the wall.

"He just walked out the front door."

The phone slipped from my fingers. I fell back and gazed at my ceiling fan in defeat. I could hear my name faintly being called through the phone. I sighed and lifted it back to my ear.

"Thanks anyway. Just tell him to call me back, I guess."

"Alright. Have a good night." I was about to hang up when she said, "If you ever need someone to talk to, I'm here."

"Okay, thanks. That's very kind of you." I would have appreciated the gesture more if I wasn't so disappointed. How would

I ever go to sleep knowing Jasper's time in Oportet was being counted down, and he wouldn't even talk to me?

I didn't feel like changing for bed, so I just lay on my back with my eyes shut. I tried to clear my mind, using the relaxation technique I created on the day of my OGS. I took each of my worries and sorted them, then locked them all away. I let each thought pass through my mind until there was almost nothing left. Everything was quiet. Everything was peaceful.

My state of calm made the noise at my window crack like a gunshot. I bolted upright, petrified as I watched the unlocked window slide open. My eyes darted around my room, looking for a weapon. They landed on the lamp on my bedside table. I shot out of bed and into action, grabbing the lamp and holding it out in front of me like a sword.

It took me a few seconds before I realized that the lamp was still plugged into the wall. I tried to jerk it out, but it was stuck on something. I frantically backed up to my door, ready to make a run for it.

"A hand please?" *Jasper.*

I crept up to the window, meeting his dark eyes with a flurry of emotions.

"I was kidding, Luna. Get out of the way." I let out a breath of relief at the humor in his voice.

He placed his palms against the windowsill, propelling himself into my room. After a few seconds of debating, I gave into my gut instinct and ran into his arms. I must have taken him by surprise, because he lost his balance and slammed into the wall, taking me with him.

I heard the thump of his head hitting the surface, followed by a stream of hushed obscenities. He placed his hands on my shoulders and gently pulled me off of him, rubbing the back of his head with a grimace.

"What was that?" Jasper muttered. "Are your parents home? That was really loud."

"No, they're at some kind of top secret government conference." I took in a breath. "You can't leave Oportet!" I blurted, watching his eyes widen.

Jasper ran a hand through his hair and intertwined his fingers with mine. He led me back to my bed, sitting next to me in silence. I felt a trail of warmth where his thumb continued to trace over my hand.

"Why didn't you tell me?"

"I didn't want you to do anything stupid."

I felt anger boiling in my chest. He'd better believe I would do something stupid for him.

"There's nothing you can do to save me."

"I'll find a way," I vowed.

Jasper shook his head. "Luna—"

"Can't we go to the Outside together? I could do something to piss off the Council and they could send me with you." I wasn't even thinking clearly anymore. I was desperate.

Jasper snapped his head around to look into my eyes, the intensity high enough for me to flinch.

"Stop. Just stop. You know that's not how it works."

I looked away.

"They would just make you forget again."

I knew he was right, but I couldn't help but imagine a life for us outside Oportet. Did I really have the guts to leave with Jasper?

"I don't want to lose you again." He lifted a hand and brushed his fingers along my cheekbones.

"I'll find a way," I repeated. "I promise."

Something heartbreaking crept into Jasper's eyes—emptiness.

"You aren't telling me something," I said.

Jasper froze, but then his face softened. He opened his mouth to speak—probably to defend himself—but decided against it.

He moved his hand off mine and lifted it to my face, successfully ridding my mind of all thoughts. I knew exactly what he was doing. I was just too weak to fight it.

"I didn't write that letter last year," I said. "My parents did."

Jasper stared at me in confusion, his forehead creasing. "What?"

"I overheard them talking about it. That's how I found out about your trial. My father said he left it on your front porch and watched you get it."

Jasper's face looked white. "Oh my god." He ran a hand through his hair. "I can't believe this."

"I don't understand...why would my parents write the letter?"

"It kind of makes sense. They hated that we were together. Wait, you don't know that yet, do you?"

I shook my head.

"Well, when they found out they went ballistic. That's when I found out just how deep the stigma against Outsiders really ran."

I nodded, but I still wasn't completely on the same page. The frustration coursed through me. I would never be on the same page. Not without my memories.

"I haven't remembered anything in a week." The anxiety was tearing me apart. Remembering was the only thing that would help me.

"What was the last thing you remembered?"

I couldn't help smiling as I thought about my last memory.

"What's that little smile for?" Jasper narrowed his eyes with curiosity.

"I remembered our first kiss."

A slight smile crept onto his lips. I felt my shoulders relax at the change of conversation topic—or maybe it was the fact that I got Jasper to smile. I was beginning to think that kind of rarity was reserved only for the past.

"Oh yeah? Awkward, right?" Jasper said.

I let out pent-up laughter.

"On the swing set...like a couple of prepubescent elementary school children."

I laughed even harder, afraid if I stopped I would start crying. I fell back on my bed, grabbing Jasper's arm and pulling him down with me.

"Why are you laughing?" he asked as I was practically convulsing next to him.

"I can't stop!" I sucked in oxygen, trying to get myself under control. What was happening? All I really wanted to do was cry, but there I was, letting out all of my anger, worry, sadness and pain into a mess of hysterical laughter, of all things. To think all it took was to be compared to a "prepubescent elementary school child" for all of my suppressed emotions to come rushing to the surface.

Jasper started laughing as he watched me gasping for air. "We are so messed up." My insides were going all kinds of crazy. Could Jasper and I really still be a *we*?

"It's fine if you don't remember everything. Don't stress over it, okay?" Jasper said without looking at me. His eyes turned glassy, his face reserved.

I went silent, studying his face. He was hiding something.

"I thought you'd want me to remember everything," I said after a few beats of quiet. I felt Jasper shrug his shoulders next to me.

"I'm just saying that it's not completely necessary now that we know the letter was from your parents. So, you know, don't strain yourself trying to force it out."

Something was wrong. He was the last person I thought wouldn't want me to have my memories back.

"Okay," I said slowly. He was making me want to compel my recollections even more than before. I didn't think I had to worry about Jasper keeping things from me, but now I was beginning to think that even he was afraid of what my memories would reveal.

"So what happened to Alex? I've only seen him in my memories."

Jasper flinched at the sound of his cousin's name.

"He was sent to the Outside." For some reason that didn't surprise me. The news still left me oddly unsettled.

"Oh...I'm sorry."

"Don't be. He deserved it." Jasper sounded distant—cold, even.

Before I could ask him what Alex did, Jasper was shifting his position so that he was leaning over me. I could feel my heart speeding as he lowered his face just above mine.

"You're so—"

Chapter Fourteen

....

"**B**eautiful," Jasper whispered as he leaned in to kiss me under the soft morning light. Muted rays of sunlight streamed in through the tall trees as we lay in our special spot in the forest.

"We're going to be late," I said, letting him leave a trail of kisses along my collarbone. I shivered at the tickling sensation. Jasper chuckled, pulling himself up and holding out a hand to help me. I took it, and didn't let go until we reached the school building.

"What a great way to start the morning," he said, grinning.

"Says the morning person. It's bad enough to get up so early for school, but I can't believe I let you talk me into getting up even earlier to take a detour!"

"Wasn't it worth it?"

I blushed. "Yes."

Before separating to get to our lockers I caught sight of Jenna. She was staring right at us, her eyes flickering to our intertwined hands for a quick moment before she turned to a huge group of kids gathered in front of her. She was waving her hands around as she spoke to Kevin McCarthy, a disturbing expression on her face.

Kevin glanced at Jasper and me, then back at her. Confirming my fears of the discussion topic, Jenna raised a finger and pointed straight at us. A couple of Kevin's friends patted him on the back—or maybe they were pushing on his back—encouraging him toward us.

"What's going on?" I whispered to Jasper.

"Nothing good." Jasper watched the group, a look of concern growing on his face. "We need to go," he said suddenly, his hand tightening around mine.

Before I could react, he was pulling me in the opposite direction. I looked over my shoulder just as Kevin reached us. He tapped on Jasper's arm, something wild in his eyes.

"Turn around, freak," Kevin commanded. Jasper let go of my hand and moved to stand in front of me, shielding me from whatever Kevin was sent to do. A wave of nausea hit me as I peeked behind the two boys to the growing crowd of students. Jenna and her group of instigators looked on expectantly.

"You don't want to do this," Jasper said. His voice was calmer than mine would have been.

"Don't you dare tell me what I want."

Jasper's jaw tensed.

"You are nothing more than the filth our walls are supposed to keep out."

"Yet here I am," Jasper fired back. "I thought you clones lived to worship your leaders. They're the ones who let me in. If you have a problem with it you can take it up with them." Jasper was in the process of turning away when Kevin slammed a fist into his jaw.

Jasper's head snapped back from the impact, appearing to be as surprised as I was. I held a hand to my mouth. Was this what Jenna wanted to happen?

The violent act sent many students into shock, some scurrying away at the sight of rules being broken, while some froze as they watched the scene unfold. Although she was far away, I could have sworn Jenna had a smug smile on her lips.

After placing a hand to the spot of impact, Jasper shook his head and laughed dryly. "You have a weak punch."

Why was he making the situation worse? Surely Jasper new that Kevin could only get more violent. Where the hell were any of the teachers? The principal's office was just down the hall. Why weren't they hearing this?

Kevin was fuming. "At least I don't prey on the weak," he snapped, looking over at me. "Why can't you see that he's brainwashing you? I bet he's already turned you against us—against Oportet."

"Actually, only people like you could turn me against anything." I fired back. "And you're one to talk about brainwashing. How about you take a second to think about why you even have these ridiculous prejudices in the first place!" My voice was rising, and I realized that everyone had gone completely silent. Even Jasper was staring at me with wide eyes. Jenna's jaw had dropped, completely stunned at my outburst. She almost looked pained, like my words were flying across the hall and hitting her in the gut. "While you're at it, you should also consider why you do anything. You don't even have a mind of your own." I looked around the hallway. "None of you do!"

"You're insane," Kevin said incredulously. "Why are you so blind?" He jabbed his finger into Jasper's chest. "He's just screwing with you. You're just too big of a desperate slut to think clearly. I guess the rumors from freshman year were true after—"

Everything happened so quickly that Kevin's final words were lost in the melee. In one fluid motion, Jasper nailed Kevin with a wide-arcing punch to the mouth, promptly knocking him on his ass. Now I knew that Jasper wasn't bluffing when he called Kevin's punch weak—that was obvious in comparison.

How did Jasper learn to hit someone like that? He had mentioned the Outside being dangerous, but I hadn't really thought about how that had affected him. I wondered how often he found it necessary to protect himself out there.

Kevin was stunned, wincing as he felt his lips, already red with blood. I hoped the strike made him bite his tongue. I had never felt so embarrassed in front of so many people in my life.

Kevin managed to stand. He looked like he wanted to murder Jasper here in the middle of the school hallway. I didn't understand how he could still have so much determination and hate in his eyes after it was clear who would come out of the battle on top. Kevin took a step forward, but a voice down the hall made every student in the hallway freeze.

"That's enough! The three of you are coming with me," said a stern woman's voice. I turned to see our vice principal, Mrs. Hamilton, staring us down, her nostrils flaring. "This little scene will demand serious repercussions."

I swallowed, terrified at how my parents would react at the news that their perfect daughter was in the middle of a school fight. It wasn't going to be pretty.

Mrs. Hamilton pointed a stubby finger at me. "And you, I heard everything you said. So did the cameras," she said with a smile full of venom. I followed her gaze to the ceiling, where one of the school's cameras was pointed right at us.

The camera was both a blessing and a curse. If it captured the incriminating things I'd said, at least it would also show who started the fight. I didn't want everyone to gang up on Jasper just because he was the easy target. I hoped the authorities would see the truth as clearly as it was captured on the tape.

~~~~~

"But Mrs. Hamilton, you don't understand. This was a hate crime. They attacked us because Jasper was an Outsider," I protested. The four of us were sitting in the vice principal's office, and Mrs. Hamilton was handing out our punishments. Jasper kept glancing my way, and

when I finally met his eyes he gave me a look to assure me that everything would be okay. I hoped he was right.

"Luna Beckham, don't you dare talk back to me. We haven't even
begun to discuss the seriousness of your indiscretions. Who started the
fight and for what reason is irrelevant. Mr. Williams used violence in
this situation, which will result in a weeklong suspension, and because
of his current citizen status, he will also be on probation." She directed
her attention back to Jasper. "You know what will happen if you mis-
behave while on probation, don't you?"

Jasper nodded.

I knew the term from my parents. If a citizen from the Outside
broke any rules while on probation they would be forced out of Oportet.
This was completely unfair to Jasper. How did the instigator get off
easier than the victim? A week of suspension alone was not enough for
what Kevin did that morning.

I cast a glance at Kevin, who was holding a bloody ice pack to his
busted lip. I didn't feel an ounce of pity.

"Luna, I do not have the grounds to suspend you because you were
not directly involved in the fighting, but personally," she leaned closer to
me over her desk, her eyes fiery, "I think what you did was far worse
than any act of violence." Something huge was exploding within me,
like all my thoughts were forming into one. I did not want to be a part
of a society that shamed free speech more than they did hatred or violence.

It was like cracks were rippling through how Oportet was por-
trayed in my mind, and they had been growing since Jasper had asked,
"Do you like it here?" at the science museum.

The answer had been "no." My life consisted of obeying, behaving,
and going through the motions, and I knew my life would continue in
that fashion until I died.

As soon as that thought formed, there was no going back. It had caused a chain reaction. Suddenly I was agreeing to meet a boy I barely knew, and then continually sneaking out to meet him. The way he carried himself, making me want, for the first time in my life, to not accept the mindlessness of Oportet, but to want something more, something that showed me the difference between existing and living—and then, once everything was set in motion, I couldn't stop the thoughts that were pushing through the walls in my mind, until all of the barriers came crashing down.

The cracks grew and grew until my entire perception of our society crumbled into oblivion. I knew what I was taught to believe in, and I knew what I had been taught to oppose, and that glaring red line between the two had faded until everything ran together.

Oportet might have been safe, but safe was neither what I wanted, nor needed, to be happy. I'd always been told that the meaning of life was to follow the rules to achieve success, order, and purpose in Oportet, but I was beginning to realize that life wasn't that simple.

I now believed the meaning of life was to find what set a person on fire, what made someone want to love unconditionally, what made someone adventurous, and what truly made a person happy. I wasn't sure exactly what would make me feel all of those things, but I wanted to find out.

"But," Mrs. Hamilton continued, "this kind of behavior will require several sessions with our school's guidance counselor. If that doesn't help you see just how wrong you are, then it's off to the Council." She said it like going to the Council was the equivalent of me jumping off of a cliff onto sharp rocks, and like she couldn't wait to watch. She pried her disdainful eyes off of me to address the three of us collectively. "The tape on the camera will be distributed to each of your parents."

Oh no. I thought I was going to throw up. If I did, then I would be sure to aim at Mrs. Hamilton.

~~~~~

Was it really necessary to include Jasper and me entering the building holding hands? I knew that Mrs. Hamilton had something to do with the way the tape was cut for our parents to view. Mine were taking it in with more anger and surprise than I even knew they possessed. Every few seconds, their heads would turn to stare at me. I tried not to meet their eyes. We were watching it on the big TV in our living room. It was humiliating. At least Megan was sent to her room before my parents slid the disc into our DVD player.

Mother gasped after my little rant about the many faults of Oportet. I'd envisioned my parents yelling at me and preaching to me about what an awful person I was, but they kept quiet, enraptured at the screen. They continued to stare for a long while after the video was over.

"Please tell me that wasn't you we were watching," *Mother whispered. Her eyes searched mine desperately.* "Please tell me that you aren't... with... an Outsider."

Now that my relationship with Jasper was no longer a secret, their disproval angered me. It wasn't like they were against dating; I knew that from their constant prodding for me to associate with the sons of big shots in high governmental positions. They were just against Jasper.

"Why would you say those things?" *Father asked.* "Although Kevin was in the wrong, he was right about one thing."

How could Father possibly defend anything Kevin did—or said?

"This Jasper is a bad influence, and as your parents we will not let it continue."

"You're so much better than this," Mother added, gesturing to the screen. She looked heartbroken.

I knew all the blame would be placed on Jasper, and no one would ever stop to think that I came to any conclusions on my own. "What I said had nothing to do with Jasper. I don't like the way Oportet is being run. It's wrong." My parents were done playing nice. I could see it on their faces.

"It doesn't matter what you think," Mother spat. "You have no idea what you're saying or thinking right now—no teenager does. You should be thankful that you live in such a wonderful place as Oportet. These rules keep you safe, and give your life a purpose." She spoke like she was reading a script from one of the few movies the Council permitted.

I had so many valid arguments I was prepared to counter her with, but then I remembered what Aunt May had said to me about them being "far too gone to be rational."

My parents were asleep, and I had to accept the fact that I did not possess the ability to wake them up. It wasn't too late for me, but sadly it was for them.

~~~~~

I hadn't seen Jasper since the fight Friday morning. It was Saturday now and my family was about to leave for Megan's soccer tournament, leaving me to "sort out the real truth from what had been implanted into my brain maliciously," as my mother put it. It was funny because that was what I had been trying to do for the past month now, although not in the manner she wanted.

I'd been keeping the upstairs phone in my room, and no one had even noticed it was missing. Most people used computers for communication, including my parents. My parents each had their own laptops. Megan and I shared one, but I rarely used it. Megan was on it nonstop video-calling her many friends. She was the it-girl of middle school. I wouldn't be surprised if she had a secret boyfriend herself.

Jasper called me late last night, and I'd agreed to meet him at his house while my family was at the fields watching back-to-back games in the miserable cold. It was forty degrees, windy, with light drizzle. Needless to say, I felt pretty damn lucky to be on house arrest for the day—not that I was planning on actually staying true to this order. I'd go crazy without contact with someone who didn't treat me like a criminal. All I'd done was speak the truth. Why was that so bad?

I braided my long, dark hair to the side. After grabbing a blue zip-up hoodie from my closet, I checked my appearance in the mirror. I scrutinized every one of my imperfections before I shook my head and walked away. The rain would ruin any makeup or hair fixes anyway. The freezing rain would be blowing into my face all the way to Jasper's house.

I might have hated the miserable trek if it didn't end with meeting Jasper. I wrapped my arms around myself, surprisingly chilled for someone who tends to thrive in the cold.

My thoughts attacked me. I might have seemed strong in that video, and I might have stood my ground with Mrs. Hamilton and my parents, but the truth was that I was scared.

I was scared that I was somehow going to get Jasper expelled from Oportet, or that all of this was just one big dream, and I would soon be brought back into the same old routine that I would live out for the rest of my life. I hated to admit it, but a small part of me feared my parents and Mrs. Hamilton were right. What if Jasper really did brainwash me without me detecting it? What if everything I'd been doing and thinking this past month was just a series of huge mistakes?

Was Jasper even capable of such a horrific scheme? I knew how my parents would answer that question. They were convinced that it was *all a part of the Outsiders' plan to infiltrate the minds of Oportet's youth to gain supporters for their cause. I had never really given much thought to what most people considered extremist conspiracy theories, but I knew that they were convinced of the Outsiders' plan to take over Oportet and take down the Council, much like what happened with the former American government.*

I didn't believe a word of it, and neither did most of the citizens of Oportet. There have been countless studies that have shown Oportet to be as much as one hundred times more stable than the American government in its final years. It would take something drastic to take down our government.

I knocked on Jasper's door, dying to get inside. I was so close to warmth it was painful. Jasper opened the door, taking me in with a look of surprise.

"What in the world...? Luna, it's awful out there. You really just walked here?" He shut the door behind me, and then pulled me against him. "God, you're frozen."

"Well it's not like I could get my parents to drive me," I said, shuddering against the warmth of his body.

He pulled away and dangled a set of car keys in front of me. "I was about to come get you. You're early."

"Oh. I'm sorry."

Jasper looked at me like I was speaking a different language. "Why are you apologizing? I'm the one who just let my girlfriend walk two miles in the cold and rain." I could hear him saying something else, but I wasn't really listening. Girlfriend. He had just called me his girlfriend. I could picture my face turning red.

Jasper must have noticed my internal freak-out because he'd stopped talking to stare at me. "What's wrong?" he asked.

What was wrong? Wasn't that what I wanted?

"Nothing," I said. Of course it was what I wanted. It was just that saying it out loud made it real. It made everything real: the fight at school, my parents' disproval, my doubts about Oportet, late night calls and sneaking out to meet Jasper, and the scariest thing of all—every feeling for him I'd ever experienced.

That was when I knew who was the real brainwasher. Jasper might have helped me wake up, but in the end it was still up to me whether or not to stay asleep, or to live and be free. He wasn't forcing me to think or feel anything. I chose.

Oportet—the Council and their rules—was what took away everyone's choice. I wanted a choice.

"Are you sure you're okay?"

I jolted out of my trance, my eyes flickering to Jasper's.

"You're acting really strange." His eyes widened. "I am so insensitive, aren't I?"

"What? Why?"

He sat me down on the living room couch, and tossed me a blanket.

"I should have asked you how it went down with your parents. I never wanted you to get into any trouble." He ran a hand through his hair.

"It wasn't your fault!" I protested, wanting to wipe the scowl off of his face. I could use one of those contagious smiles right about now.

"And what he said..."

Now it was my turn to look away. I had tried to suppress the memory of being called a desperate slut in front of whole school.

"He was just trying to lash out at me, and maybe a little at you for choosing the wrong side." He gave me a weak smile. "And I swear it was never my goal to try to... force... any of my beliefs on you. I just thought you were already... like me."

"Trust me, I know Kevin was full of shit. I also know he was trying to drive a stake between us, probably for Jenna." I felt a stab of anger thinking about how cold Jenna had turned. She was my best friend only weeks ago. "I can't believe she pushed Kevin into starting that fight."

Jasper stiffened at the sudden sound of voices from the foyer. He shook his head and muttered something under his breath.

"I thought your mother worked at the grocery store on Saturdays," I said, hearing a female voice matched with Alex's.

"She does."

I got up to see the commotion, ignoring Jasper's protests to stay in the living room. He followed me closely.

My eyes widened when I reached Alex—and a blonde I didn't recognize. Alex was wearing sunglasses and a hoodie as he came down the stairs, and the girl was wearing a freakishly small dress for her curvy figure, her mascara smeared like she'd slept in it.

"What the hell?" I mumbled quietly. Who wears sunglasses indoors?

The blonde was giggling like a maniac, touching an unresponsive Alex's arm as she whispered to him. I didn't see how he was hearing her with his hood up like that.

"Oh, is this your brother?" she squealed. "What a gene pool!"

I couldn't help but let out a small laugh at her enthusiasm.

"How are you still buzzed?" Alex moaned, reaching under his sunglasses to rub his eyes.

Well that made sense. I had never consumed alcohol before, but I'd heard of kids who had broken the rule that forbid anyone from getting drunk or of the possession of alcohol by those below the age of twenty-five.

The blonde's eyes landed on me. "Who's that? Is that your sister?"

AWAKEN

"She's at my house enough to be my sister," Alex muttered. The girl waved at me crazily, and I gave her a small wave back.

"You're pretty!" she yelled, awkwardly fumbling down the steps. Alex clamped his hands over his ears.

"What did I tell you about screaming in my ear?" Alex growled. He opened the front door, ushering her out.

"Call me!" she whispered loudly, waving goodbye to all of us with a big smile. Her breasts were practically popping out of her red dress.

"He won't," I heard Jasper say behind me, earning him a glare from Alex.

"Of course, babe," Alex said with absolutely zero emotion. Actually, that wasn't true—the annoyance was detectable, at least to me. The girl seemed content with his answer, and turned to say something else when Alex shut the door in her face.

"What the hell, Alex?" Jasper moved to stand next to me. "She can't drive like that."

"She doesn't have a car, you moron. I drove her here." Alex said it like we were with him the whole time.

"And you're not driving her back...to wherever she came from?" I was glad to hear as much disgust in Jasper's voice as I was feeling towards Alex.

"She's fine to walk."

I gawked at him incredulously. Was he being serious? Jasper grabbed his keys, shoving past Alex.

"Dude. She lives in our neighborhood. Chill." Alex started walking back up the stairs. "At least I think she's the one who does." He shrugged and disappeared into his room.

~~~~~

133

We were on the way back from dropping off the blonde, who we learned was named Sophie, and I was growing more and more unsettled.

"Is everyone on the Outside like Alex?" I blurted. Jasper glanced at me from the driver's seat and sighed.

"I'm not like that, am I?"

I shook my head.

"Just because you have a choice doesn't mean you'll make the wrong one. We might not have ironclad rules out there, but everyone doesn't choose to be like Alex. I think most people are inherently benevolent, at least for the most part. The rest are screwed up by cruel circumstances."

"Was Alex?"

"His father was a drunk. My mom kind of kidnapped him when he was barely a teenager, and I say 'kind of' because Alex was very willing to get away from his abusive father. But the damage was done. We took him with us to Oportet, but he was already too messed up." We were now in the driveway, neither of us getting out of the car.

"Is that why you came here? For him?"

Jasper shook his head. "No." He looked away, taking in a deep breath. I could see that he was preparing himself to say something— something important. "My dad was shot," he said finally.

I stared at him in disbelief.

"My mom brought us here because she was scared. She wanted us to be safe. Oportet is safe."

"I'm so sorry," I breathed. I wasn't sure what to do, or what to say. I leaned over and wrapped my arms around him, and he leaned into me. I rested my head on his shoulder.

"Come on," Jasper whispered. "I'm tired of all this heaviness. Let's go do something light for once."

I pulled away. "Like what?"

"A zombie apocalypse movie," he said, the corners of his mouth tipping upwards.

I rolled my eyes, already quite familiar with Jasper's obsession with zombie movies. They were my least favorite of his illegal stash, but if they made him happy, then I was all in. He'd just better believe we were watching one of Lilly's vampire movies next.

Chapter Fifteen

....

A hand moved in front of my face. I was lying on my back, my body motionless but my eyes wide open. I heard Jasper's voice like it was at the other end of some tunnel.

"Luna? What the hell is going on?"

I sat up. "Alex is a mess," I mumbled, seeing Jasper flinch like before at the mention of Alex. I moved to a sitting position.

"You were freaking me out! It was like you were somewhere else.... Well, I guess you were." He exhaled slowly. "What did you remember?" he asked with caution.

"Getting in trouble for the fight with Kevin, me having some kind of epiphany about the meaning of life," I said.

Jasper smirked.

"And Alex with some random drunk girl," I finished.

Jasper nodded, seeming to recall those events himself.

"Kevin. I remember that asshole," he muttered.

"And now, so do I."

Jasper smiled. "You know, I kind of wish I could relive these memories through your eyes. It has always been so infuriating for me to try and figure out what is going on in that head of yours."

"Um, I don't even know what is going on in this head of mine. I thought I had everything figured out until I started getting these memories back. Now I'm realizing how screwed up everything is—apparently for a second time."

"Are all of the epiphanies wearing you out?" Jasper laughed.

They definitely weren't making my brain any less confused.

"I'm sorry," Jasper said suddenly.

"Why are you sorry?"

"You were right that day we spoke outside of the middle school."

I furrowed my brows trying to remember what I was right about.

"I was playing the victim when I shouldn't have been. I can't imagine what it would be like to go through what you have."

"That was before I knew about the letter you thought I wrote. You had a right to be angry, and it made perfect sense why you were so hurt. It has been killing me to think that you went that many months thinking I'd written something so heartless."

Jasper was staring at my open window, and I desperately wanted to know what he was thinking about. "Well, in your defense, the letter didn't sound anything like you. I guess I'd gone so long thinking that you were too good to be true, that when you said all of those things about coming to your senses, it was what I'd been anticipating the whole time."

That wasn't at all what I'd expected. "You have got to be joking," I scoffed.

Jasper narrowed his eyes, and I could sense his frustration at my reaction.

"I thought you knew me better than that." I still had the remainder of the school year's worth of memories before the major fallout went down, which meant we would have been close for more than seven months. Yet he relied on his own insecurities instead of everything he had ever learned about me from our time together.

"I thought I did, Luna! I wanted to fight for you, or at least hear you say those things to me in person, but every time I called or knocked on your door your parents said you didn't want to speak to me. I even came to some of your speeches railing against your rebellious phase and how you were recovering from it. I guess you were just too convincing."

I couldn't speak. I had no idea that Jasper had put himself through all of that for me.

"I didn't know what went wrong—or what I did wrong—for you to completely change overnight. You wanted nothing to do with me, and you were suddenly the ghost of the girl I used to love."

I winced, his words sending all kinds of pain through my system.

"I'd been keeping my distance all summer, and then one day I decided to talk to you in the parking lot after your Oportet Day speech, and you looked straight through me. I could *feel* that you had forgotten me."

"Jasper." I turned to look at him, willing him to meet my eyes. When he finally did, I had to hold myself together with whatever I had left. His eyes shined like glass—and never in my life could I handle seeing Jasper cry because of the pain I had caused him. "I am so sorry. I don't remember everything, but I'm beginning to, and I can honestly swear to you that I would never choose to forget you. *Never.*"

"I know," he whispered.

I lost all of my thoughts as he leaned closer to me, and everything I was going to say disappeared with them.

He tucked my hair behind my ears, making me feel vulnerable without the long dark strands to hide my face.

"When do your parents get back from the conference?" Jasper asked. Megan was staying at her best friend Stacy's house for the weekend. Stacy was an only child so her parents were more than happy to help. My parents wanted me to stay with Jenna, forcing me to have a very awkward conversation about how Jenna and I were no longer friends. I tried to stay vague, dodging all of Mother's prying questions.

"Sunday night." It was Friday, and they had left a few hours ago. My parents had been extremely secretive about the whole thing, so I knew something big was going down within the government. "Do you want something to eat? Or drink?" I asked, feeling rude considering we could go anywhere in the empty house.

"Wow. I don't think I've ever been anywhere except your room," Jasper said.

He had been in my room before? I blushed, fearing what my mind hid from me.

"I could give you a tour, if you want," I offered, thankful we had moved on from talking about things that made us cry.

"No, um, I should go," Jasper said.

I nodded, trying not to look as disappointed as I felt. "Okay." I watched as he made it to the window, and then hesitated.

"I forgot something," he said finally. He turned and came back to me, placing his hands on either side of my face and pulling me in for a kiss.

It was over too quickly, and after giving me a sad smile, he climbed out the window.

"You know you can just go out the front door, right?"

"Yeah, but it makes me look cooler this way. More badass."

I laughed, but I knew that the sound was only heard by me. Jasper was gone.

~~~~~

Mother called to check in on me, rambling on about how proud of me she was for changing my ways, no doubt in response to whatever Tomlinson had told them about Jasper approaching me. Everyone was trying hard to keep Jasper and me apart, and no one seemed to suspect anything suspicious from my end... yet. This secret had an expiration date though; I could feel it. I also had a feeling that date would coincide with the conclusion of Jasper's trial. There was no way I was just going to sit around and wait for them to throw him back to the Outside.

"So have you decided?" Mother asked, not even attempting to tone down the expectancy in her voice.

"Yes." I took a breath. "I want to be a teacher. An English teacher." I heard silence on the other line, and I could feel the irrational guilt for disappointing her. I knew it was my choice—my life—but I hated letting my parents down. They had dreamed of me working in the government since before conception. As long as I lived in Oportet, I was doing what I wanted. I was already being restricted enough.

"That's wonderful, sweetie," she said softly. "I'm very proud of you for getting this far in life."

"Thanks. Me too."

"Don't forget to call the Occupational Placement Office to let them know of your decision. You could come to work with me one day and tell them in person." The last sentence sounded more like a question, and I couldn't help but wince at the hopefulness in her voice. Taking a tour of the Council's evil lair sounded far from appealing, and it definitely wouldn't change my mind.

"Oh, no thank you. I need to call them soon anyway. I was planning on taking care of it tomorrow, before you got back. I wouldn't want to inconvenience anyone."

"I'm sure they could wait just one more day, Luna. Don't be silly."

I sighed in defeat. Fine. "Okay. I guess I could do that."

"Great!" she squealed.

I couldn't remember the last time my mother sounded that excited. I imagined she was already working on an elaborate scheme as we spoke to ensure I chose her dream job instead of mine.

Suddenly Mother started speaking very quickly. "Oh, and I don't think I would be able to take you in until *next* Monday. Sorry sweetie, the Council has just enacted something huge, so I'll be swamped this week. I have to go, bye!"

I caught myself smiling at Mother's sly maneuver.

Nothing was going to get in the way of her dream of becoming the most powerful family in Oportet. Nothing except me—I had been tearing that dream at the seams since the day I got in that school fight. I couldn't stop now.

"See you Sunday," I murmured as the phone beeped, signaling she had hung up.

I hadn't heard from Jasper since last night, and I was beginning to doubt myself. I thought I had read the situation correctly—that Jasper was finally coming around to trusting me again, especially now that he knew I never broke up with him or hurt him in that letter—but there was also the possibility that our relationship was broken beyond repair. It had been months since the accident, which meant his cynical view of me wouldn't be easy to shake off. He had lived through months of thinking I didn't love him, and if he had believed the fake letter as much as he had appeared to earlier that week, he would have gone months thinking I never loved him at all.

I could not imagine what that must have felt like, and I hadn't yet remembered our entire past. Would I really trade places with Jasper if I could? I was sure that Jasper would have given anything to forget me during the last few months, while I lost him against my will. As I was remembering everything we had been through together, Jasper had been trying his hardest to forget.

If things could ever return to how they were, it would take time. Patience was already one of my weakest qualities, but the thought of having to wait for Jasper, of all things, made me want to bang my head against the wall. We were both digging up old feelings, but the crucial difference was that it had been exciting for me, and painful for Jasper.

A whole day had passed since I had last seen him, and the amount of days I would be able to see him might be heartbreakingly limited.

I sipped my peach tea, staring out of the kitchen window. The clouds were dark and heavy, indicating the impending storm. I felt like there were many storms approaching, and they were far worse than the lightning and thunder forming within those clouds.

My vision blurred, as if I was crying. I turned my head in the direction of movement in my peripheral. Suddenly my parents were standing next to me, their mouths moving furiously with the absence of sound. I dropped my cup of tea, barely sensing the hot water burn me through my clothes.

I grabbed a handful of napkins from behind me on the table, dabbing myself and trying to ignore my parents. They weren't really there—at least not in the present. My parents were standing next to me, chastising me as I stared out the window *last year*.

Giving up on cleaning my mess, I sat back in the chair and squeezed my eyes tightly. My mind was having a spaz attack as it tried to decipher what was happening in the present versus what was happening in the memory.

I took relaxing breaths, finally tuning in to the words coming from my parents' mouths.

Chapter Sixteen

....

"**W**hat the hell happened to you, Luna?" I'd heard Father curse before, but only in extreme situations. He'd never cursed at me, and I was surprised how it resembled a punch to the stomach. "After all the trouble you caused yesterday, you really had the nerve to push it further? And don't you dare think for a minute that we don't know where you went."

"I just went for a walk," I lied. I still hated lying to my parents, but I was scared of what might happen to Jasper if they knew the whole truth—that I would never stop seeing him, even if it meant sneaking out. It was no secret that my parents could get rid of an Outsider if they really wanted to, and it would be even easier now that Jasper was on probation.

"You will be attending every one of your sessions with the school counselor, and if you don't snap out of this ridiculous phase after that, then we will have to seek additional guidance from the Council. I've known kids who have really benefited from the Council's help. Remember Don Hensley?"

I sucked in a breath, remembering our neighbor's oldest son, Don, who my parents referred to as a troublemaker throughout his teenage years. He had to go through a form of rehabilitation to get him "back on track." I remembered my parents congratulating the family at a dinner party—Don's parents wearing triumphant smiles as if Don had recovered from a chronic disease—but the most haunting thing I remembered was the look in Don's eyes. They were two voids—empty of passion, wonder, love, and life. He was hollow. I barely recognized the former outgoing and sociable boy who had lived next door since before I was born. That version of Don was gone.

"I will go to every session," I promised. I would not end up like Don Hensley. I would not let the council destroy me like they did him.

~~~~~

School was ten times worse without Jasper. I kept catching myself glancing at his empty chair during math, as if he would materialize out of thin air.

Jenna had traded seats a few weeks ago, making it blatantly obvious that she wanted nothing to do with me anymore. I now sat next to a quiet, pale blonde with glasses. I could imagine how easy it was for Jenna to manipulate the poor girl to get the seat she wanted.

It was Thursday, and I had spent a lot of time at Aunt May's house that week. She listened to me, and gave me valuable advice—something I needed at the moment. At school, I either received zero eye contact or intense stares from my classmates. Even those who didn't witness the hallway fight heard multiple accounts of it over the weekend. I was the talk of the school, and no one was on my side.

Well, Jasper was on my side. He didn't care who I rebelled against, or if I rebelled at all. My parents had been trying to convince me of his hidden agenda—of all the Outsiders' hidden agendas—to revolt against the government and overthrow the Council. I just feigned shock and let her believe that I was hanging on every word she said.

Her paranoia had been at an all time high since she saw the school footage. She was convinced that all of the Outsiders had banned together, and they were now targeting gullible teenagers to recruit to their side. Because my parents had connections within the government, she claimed that it made perfect sense why they would target me.

~~~~~

146

"Do you think that Mother is right?" I asked Aunt May, seated in her elegant living room for the third time this week. "About the group of rebel Outsiders, I mean."

"I honestly wouldn't say the idea was that far-fetched," May said. She noticed my raised eyebrow and continued. "I have met my fair share of immigrants from the Outside. They don't come because they believe in the Council's teachings. They come for protection."

Now I was even more confused.

"The reason people have relied on government for so many years is because the ultimate purpose of any government is to protect its people. It keeps order by creating laws, or rules, that keep people from running wild on the streets. Rules protect citizens from other citizens."

Like what happened to Jasper's father. There were no rules to protect him from his killer. "I don't understand. If Outsiders came here for order, then wouldn't they be content with the way things are being run?"

"Not necessarily. Do you know how Oportet was formed so quickly after the fallout?" she asked. "Maybe Jasper told you?"

I shook my head, trying my hardest to understand what she was telling me.

"The Council was created by a handful of the most powerful politicians that held office at the time of the great fallout. They wanted to form the perfect society, with the perfect rules, and the perfect way to live—the perfect way to control the masses. That was how Oportet was formed.

"They used the very ideals that led to the American government's own destruction, amplified them in a way they never could have with America's protection of rights, and watched as concerned citizens flocked from all over to be a part of this ultimate utopia, the society with the most civil—and protected—citizens in this country. The only problem: this utopia leaves no power to the citizens.

"The Council controls everything to ensure there are minimal acts of rebellion and doubt. Limiting what we watch, what we read, what we listen to, and what we are allowed to say all serve to ensure the Council remains in power. It's all a perfectly orchestrated scheme to keep, and even increase, the power the top politicians had when they ran the American government. Except now they have triple the power as leaders of Oportet because they don't have to worry about pesky freedoms and rights to get in the way of their agenda."

My mind was reeling. I was only absorbing a fraction of the information she was giving me. I felt like my head was about to explode.

"So Outsiders don't like the Council because they are a heightened version of the flaws in the old American government? The government that collapsed on itself?"

"Exactly."

"How do you know all of this?" It seemed like this kind of knowledge wouldn't be open to the public. I wouldn't put it past the Council to throw Aunt May to the Outside just for knowing their catastrophic secret. Members of Oportet's Council were the very same leaders who ran America into the ground, and now they were the government officials who were lying, scheming and controlling the people of Oportet in order to stay in power.

She pursed her lips. "I'm afraid I can't tell you that, dear. And I trust that you understand how imperative it is for you not to repeat this to anyone?"

I would never do anything to hurt Aunt May, and I was flattered that she trusted me enough to talk to me about such things. "Of course." I had so many questions swirling around in my head. "Wait, why don't Outsiders just tell everyone all of this? Wouldn't that be the most effective way to turn Oportet's citizens against the Council?"

"When Outsiders come to Oportet, they are given a strict set of rules to follow pertaining to what they can and can't say. They are essentially forbidden to discuss anything about the Outside, or they would be sent straight back to where they came from."

I thought about Christopher, the elementary school kid who was brutally paddled for talking about his hometown. It made sense that Outsiders would be forbidden from speaking of their old lives.

"And who would listen to them?" May continued. "You know what it's like reasoning with your parents. Now imagine what it would be like for Jasper to reason with them."

The thought of that scene alone was cringe-worthy.

"And I'm afraid there is a more pressing issue we must iron out," May said.

I tapped my fingers erratically on the arm of the chair as she swallowed her tea. There was a tight feeling in my chest, like all of the newfound information was crushing against me.

"Your mother shouldn't be so concerned with the Outsiders. They come for protection, remember? I'll bet the Council and their ways are common knowledge on the Outside, so Outsiders would know what they were getting themselves into before they even arrived. The people who your mother should be concerned about are not those who have been awake to the truth this whole time, but those who were asleep and suddenly woke up. People like you and me."

The way she was looking at me made me nervous. Maybe I was awake to the truth, but that didn't mean I had the guts to do anything about it. What could even be done?

My entire world was literally falling apart. Everything I had ever been told was a lie, and every rule I had ever obeyed was for the sole purpose of keeping me in the dark. It was terrifying. I could never un-learn the truth, and I never wanted to, but it changed everything.

It was like taking off a pair off heavily tinted sunglasses. After the initial blinding sensation, I could see everything so much clearer, with colors hitting me with a kind of amazing vividness—but the brightness also hurt my eyes. I wanted to put my sunglasses back on to protect them, and at the same time I wanted to enjoy the clarity my true sight gave me.

"I know it's a lot to take in. I wouldn't be telling you this if I didn't think you were ready to hear it, Luna."

I nodded.

"I always knew that you were different," May said quietly. "You're the reason I stayed this long."

"What do you mean? You were going to leave Oportet?" Choosing to go to the Outside was unheard of.

"I might have. I still had a lot of things to take care of..." May trailed off, lost in her own thoughts.

"How do you do it? How do you leave?"

May smiled sadly. "I'm afraid you can't."

I was surprised at how much May's answer disappointed me.

"A few close friends of mine met with the Council and requested to be set free. You know what happened?" May shook her head, a pained laugh escaping her lips. "They came back from the meeting with their minds completely changed. It was a complete one-eighty. They told us," May faltered, "told me, that it was a lot better to be confined in Oportet than to be in constant danger on the Outside. It was unreal."

"What happened to them?" My stomach was filled with unease, and I could sense that the Council had everything to do with the feeling. It reminded me of what happened to Don.

"I couldn't tell you. They stopped talking to me, telling me they were tired of my conspiracy theories and naivety. I'm not sure how, but the Council sure did shut them up."

"So as long as the Council runs Oportet, there's no way to get out of here," I reasoned.

Something flickered in May's eyes.

"That is correct." I detected something strange in her voice, like she was not telling the whole truth, but what reason would she have to lie?

~~~~~

We had one more school week until fall break, and Jasper and I were already planning for an epic week. We had to stay under the radar at school because of how my parents felt about our relationship. Mother probably had at least a dozen of my teachers employed as her personal spies, so we basically ignored each other until our usual walk home.

Today we walked to Jasper's house after school. Jasper, Lilly and I were all gathered in the living room in front of a small flat-screen television.

"This movie is going to make me kill myself with this fork," Jasper said, waving the utensil he had found wedged between couch cushions. Jasper claimed Alex had to have been the culprit considering how much of a slob he was.

I burst out laughing as the serious romantic vampire scene unfolded in the background.

"Shut up, Jasper," Lilly said from the chair next to us. "We're watching them all, and I don't even care if Luna has to be back home before we finish. I'm going to make you watch the whole saga with me regardless." She smiled, and I watched as Jasper held the fork between his closed eyes.

"Goodbye cruel world," he said, opening one eye to glance at me. "Are you just going to let me stab myself?"

I rolled my eyes and swatted the fork out of his hands.

"Seriously shut up or I will stab you with the fork myself," Lilly said. I couldn't help but giggle at the seriousness in her voice. There was no joking when it came to her favorite vampire movies.

Jasper crossed his arms and stayed relatively quiet throughout the remainder of the first movie. Every once in a while he turned to me and repeated whatever the actors had just said, dramatically making fun at each of their cheesy mannerisms. At one point Lilly threw a pillow at him.

I found his impressions quite amusing, but I didn't dare laugh. Jasper had told me how much Lilly liked me, and I did not want to ruin that blossoming relationship. I shot him half-hearted glares instead, catching Lilly smile in my peripheral on more than one occasion.

I thought that Lilly and May would make great friends. They were close to the same age, and they both had a way of making the best out of horrid situations. They were eternal optimists.

Lilly was the youngest mother I had ever encountered, having had Jasper in her late teens. Jasper told me that his father never left, even though a lot of men would have in that situation. They raised him against all odds, and they never stopped loving each other—staying together until his father's death.

I could still see the love Jasper spoke of in Lilly's eyes. It was there every time she looked at him, every time she listened to him speak, and every time she watched Jasper and me together when she thought we didn't notice. Many people would crumble under the weight of such a loss, but Lilly was strong. The love she had for her son made her strong.

"I should be getting home soon," I said after the second movie was over. My parents thought I was at the library studying. I was expected to be home in an hour, and as much as I loved spending time with Lilly, I also wanted to leave room for time alone with Jasper.

I had never experienced the feeling of being connected to someone on such a profound level. I felt like I could talk to Jasper about anything, and even the longest conversations with him were not enough. The fact that Jasper came from the Outside, that my parents despised him, and that every force in the universe was against us seemed to fade into the background when I was with him. I was starting to finally understand what love was.

I always thought of love as just something I would have with the person I was destined to marry, or what everyone felt automatically towards family members. I did believe I loved my family, but it was a different kind of love.

I knew that my parents loved me, but that love was tainted by all of the expectations placed upon me as a citizen of Oportet. My obedience and loyalty to the rules and to the Council was put first, and everything else a distant second. If my happiness interfered with the Council's agenda, then my parents were not capable of siding with me over their leaders. It was how they were raised, how their parents were raised, and how they had set out to raise me.

I did not want to have that kind of conditional love. I did not want to have relationships that could be completely destroyed because I thought differently, or lived differently.

The love I knew I felt for Jasper was something that was both instantaneous and gradual. I was drawn to him from the start, but the feeling only grew as time went on. It was not something that I could have stopped, that kind of effort would have been hopeless. It was an irretrievable and unconditional feeling; it made me want to learn every detail of his heart, and to hear about every thought his mind had ever conceived.

I knew it had only been a few months, but to me it felt like years. I was closer to him than I had ever been with Jenna, and I knew why. It was the same reason I didn't feel as connected to my family as I did Jasper. I didn't have to filter anything or bury any part of me. Jasper accepted me in my entirety, without any conditions, and I did the same for him.

Yet, even with the love I knew I had found with Jasper, I could still feel a haunting feeling in my chest, like it could all go up in flames. As much as I tried to brush off the feeling as an irrational fear, it persisted to nag at me.

Returning back to the life I had before I met Jasper seemed impossible, and so utterly painful that I had to push the thought from my mind.

"What are you thinking about?" Jasper asked as we cut through the forest.

"A lot of things."

He looked over at me curiously, the corners of his mouth tipping upward. "I can tell. You have your thinking face on. Should I be worried?"

I laughed to reassure him. I could worry about my confusing emotions enough for the both of us. "I think too much. That's my ultimate flaw." I sighed, trying to shake out all of the annoying, irrational worries and doubts from my head.

"I could help you with that if you wanted."

I looked at him quizzically, pushing through the branches to the abandoned playground. "And how could you do that?"

His mischievous smirk was unsettling. He stood in front of me studying my face, making me suddenly self-conscious.

He lowered his eyes to my lips, and I was becoming aware of exactly how he planned to clear my head. I also knew firsthand how effective a method it was.

Jasper leaned down to kiss me, his hands on my waist, holding me close to him. I could almost feel an instantaneous release of all my tension. With my recent altered perception of Oportet, I could not stop worrying about what the future would hold. Would I try to find a way out of living here, or for the rest of my life would I be trapped in a place with lies and deceit piled as high as its leaders' thirst for power?

That single thought was the hardest to let go of, but I managed it with my body so close to Jasper's. With all of the uncertainties, I held on to the fact that I still had Jasper in my future. I couldn't think of anything that would change that truth.

I pulled away, resting my forehead on his. Even with the autumn chill in the air, I had a kind of warmth inside me—and it wasn't from my favorite gray sweater.

Jasper had the faintest of smiles on his lips, the kind that made me believe we were invincible, that nothing was powerful enough to stop us. It was the kind of smile that validated every thought of hope I had ever possessed, that somehow, we would be able to escape the fate that had been placed on me since my birth. It made me believe that we could somehow break free, even when no one else had.

We would find freedom. I did not know when or how, but I knew that was my future. My future was liberation.

Chapter Seventeen

I was still sitting in the chair. It had only taken me a minute to recover several weeks worth of memories.

I felt lost. I'd been so hopeful and optimistic about my future last year, and it was heartbreaking to know just how wrong I had been. Hope was no match for what the Council would do to maintain order. My future had not been liberation; it continued to be imprisonment. I remained trapped, and I hadn't a clue how to free myself.

I finished cleaning up the tea I spilled before the memory then made my way to the staircase. Even when I was home alone I could not break the habit of locking myself up in my bedroom.

Before I could reach the second step, I heard a knock at the door. I turned on my heel and went to the front of the house, peering out the window by the door.

I didn't realize how much I wanted it to be Jasper until I recognized Megan's face looking back at me through the glass. I let out a heavy sigh before I opened up the door, Megan tilting her head away from me as she scurried past.

"Megan?"

She didn't turn as she hurried up the stairs. "Yes, I know I'm early, and no, I don't want to talk," she said, her voice raspy and strained.

I followed her upstairs, ignoring her protests. She sat down on her bed and didn't bother closing her door. She knew me too well to think I would let her be.

"Megan, what's wrong?" I asked, sitting down next to her. I traced circles on her back, comforting her like Aunt May had always comforted me.

"I don't think you would understand," Megan said quietly.

"And why is that?"

"You've changed. You're perfect now."

I sighed, knowing I was caught between keeping my secret and comforting my sister. "No one is perfect, Megan. You can tell me anything, and I swear to keep it just between the two of us." I could tell Megan was debating whether or not to confide in me, her forehead creased in thought as tears rolled down her cheeks. She quickly wiped them away with her sleeve.

"Why would you do that? That's against the rules."

I knew the answer to that question, but somehow my mind could not conjure it up into words.

"Because I love you, Megan. You're my little sister," I said finally. Megan looked at me, crying even harder. Her slim shoulders were shaking with each sob.

"I did something bad, Luna. Now Stacy hates me," she managed, barely able to get the words out.

"What did you do?"

"I said that I wished that we didn't have any rules."

I tried to keep my face unchanged. I would have never thought Megan to be the kind of person to say things against the rules. She had always seemed so dedicated, so obedient. Then again, so had I.

"Why did you say this?"

"I don't know. It was stupid. I just, well, I have a friend who came from the Outside, and she let me listen to her music. We also watched some movies and read some stories. At first I was just curious. Melanie has always been so nice to me, so I just went along with it and promised myself that it wouldn't change anything. I knew I was breaking rules, but I just wanted to know what was so bad about the Outside. I know that it was a terrible thing to do, but..." Megan took a sharp intake of breath, a fat tear escaping her eye and rolling down her cheek. "I don't know how to explain it, Luna. Everything was just so much more emotional and just, really, really, beautiful. I don't understand why we aren't allowed to *feel* in Oportet. I just don't get it. Is it wrong to want to feel something?" She searched my eyes like they would give her all the answers.

"No," I said finally. "Having emotions is natural, but watching and reading things that make you feel the wrong emotions is dangerous." For the first time since I started regaining memories, I hated keeping it a secret.

I watched as the light in Megan's eyes faded away with each of my words. I had no other choice; the memory-wiped version of me would say these things. The old me—the version of me that triggered the Council into action—wasn't safe to reveal to anyone until I figured out the details of last year.

"Don't worry, I won't tell Mother or Father about this if you promise not to break those rules again. I know that whatever the Outsider showed you seemed good—*intoxicating*—I've been there, remember? But they are forbidden for a reason. The Council always has our best interests at heart."

"How would you know how *intoxicating* the stuff from the Outside is? You don't remember any of it," Megan retorted, obviously only listening to that one slip-up.

I faltered, trying to think of anything to pull me out of the hole I had dug. Megan stared at me intently as I fumbled.

"Well, I can guess." I took in a breath. "Regardless, you know what you did was wrong."

Megan looked away, visibly flustered. What kind of answer was she expecting from me?

"You were so different last year," Megan murmured.

"I caused a lot of needless trouble. I was being selfish and ignorant, and I don't want you making those same mistakes." I despised every word that came out of my mouth. I just wanted Megan to be happy, and I didn't care if that meant breaking some rules to get there.

"When you hit your head and forgot everything I was... *relieved*. Everyone was. Even you." Megan paused, once again meeting my eyes. "I'm starting to wonder if that was wrong, if all of it was wrong." Megan was hinting at something deeper, and I thought I knew what it was.

Was Megan feeling guilty about keeping Tomlinson's secret? The scheme to wipe me of my memories? I willed her to come out and say it, to confirm what I had been suspecting all along, but she remained quiet.

The phone ringing in the hallway startled me, and I saw Megan smiling out of the corner of my eye at my jumpiness.

I got up to answer it, casting a final glance at my sister, whom I had just misled greatly. I hoped I would someday have the chance to tell her how I really felt.

"Hello?" I said into the phone.

"Hey."

I felt a smile growing on my lips at the sound of Jasper's voice.

"You should come over and save me from doing chores." His voice sounded faraway and slightly muffled.

"Oh, is that why you called? I'm flattered that you rank me above washing dishes."

"I rank you above cleaning my room and running the vacuum too," he joked. Somehow the humor of his words didn't make it to his voice.

After an awkward beat of silence I laughed, turning to make sure Megan was still in her room. She was. "Okay. I'll be over in ten minutes."

"No, um, I can pick you up." He paused. "It's about to rain, anyway."

"Thanks." Things seemed strained. Jasper went months without talking to me or thinking I cared about him, so I could understand why our relationship starting up again would be weird for him.

"Yeah, so, I'll see you then," he said mumbled.

I was unaccustomed to anything less than ease with our conversations. "See you then," I repeated before hanging up. I shook my head and left to get ready. I hoped hanging out at his house would be less uncomfortable than that phone conversation.

I left my hair down, replaced my sweatpants with jeans, and threw on a floral print sweater. I was in the process of putting on mascara when I heard a knock at the door.

"Shit," I muttered. Jasper didn't know that Megan came home early, and I would be completely screwed if she saw Jasper at the door.

I flew to the stairs, noticing Megan slowly making her way out of her room.

"Oh, well, I guess you got that." Megan gave me a small smile and retreated back through her door.

I let out a breath of relief. I wasn't sure what I would have done if Megan saw Jasper at the door.

"Get in the car, you lunatic," I muttered, earning a raised eyebrow from Jasper. "Megan came home early from Stacy's. You're lucky I beat her to the door."

"Well that would have been a good thing to know."

"I forgot. Sue me."

Expecting a smirk, I peered over at an uncharacteristically rigid Jasper. He made his way to the passenger's side to open the door for me.

"Such a gentleman," I said.

"I find that girls dig that sort of thing." He swung into the driver's seat, and then sped off down the road. My heart lurched at the sudden acceleration.

"God, Jasper. You are going to get pulled over... if we don't *die* first."

Jasper gave me a forced smile, the kind of smile that didn't make it to his eyes. "Calm down, we'll be fine."

Jasper looked edgier than he did a year ago. His jawline seemed sharper, his hair messier and more grown out, and the circles under his eyes seemed a shade darker.

Jasper pulled into his driveway, and he made no move to exit the car. I was tapping my fingers on my leg absent-mindedly, stopping when I noticed him watching me.

"Luna, I need to tell you something."

I looked over at him, noticing how he wouldn't look me in the eyes. "Yes?"

I could feel my heart speeding up and my stomach churning, warning me that whatever Jasper needed to tell me wasn't good.

I looked out the window, and all of a sudden felt grass tickling my feet. I gasped, looking down to see if anything was rubbing up against them.

"What is it?" I heard Jasper ask, but it was like he was asking me from half a football field away.

I felt my feet moving forward through the grass, getting closer and closer to Jasper's door. I was also aware of my body that was sitting back in the car seat.

Jasper was saying something else, but it was lost in my mind's abyss as it tuned into the memory, leaving Jasper and the present behind.

Chapter Eighteen

....

I waited outside the door, hoping to surprise Jasper. It was the first official day of winter break, and I couldn't think of a better way to spend my time. My parents worked during the day, and Megan was off doing things with her friends, so it would be almost too easy for Jasper and me to hang out all week. I thought I remembered Jasper saying he was home Saturday, but I honestly wasn't that sure.

"Well, look who it is," Alex said when he opened the door. He gave me a crooked smile as he let me in. "Hot dress. It really complements your figure."

I rolled my eyes and crossed my arms, not enjoying where his eyes lingered.

"Where's Jasper?" I snapped.

He put his hands up in front of him, detecting the annoyance in my voice. "What's so great about him, anyway?" Alex took a clumsy step towards me, and that's when I smelled the alcohol. It practically radiated from his body.

"Are you really drunk right now? It's eleven o'clock in the morning, Alex."

He narrowed his eyes at me before it dissolved into a sloppy grin. "I told him you'd come to me in the end. I didn't even have to work for it!" Alex exclaimed, his speech jumbled. "And here you are..."

Alex grabbed my arm, and I recoiled against his touch.

"Hey now," he slurred.

"Seriously, stop. I didn't come here for—"

"Shut up," Alex groaned, dragging both words out longer than necessary. He was getting on my nerves even more than usual. "Just go with it. Don't fight it."

Don't' fight what? What the hell was he talking about?

Alex tugged on my wrist, bringing my body close to his. His arms circled me. Until that moment, I had never really noticed how huge he really was. I brought my hands up to his chest and pushed hard against his brick wall of pure muscle, but even in his inebriated state, he was too strong for me. Suddenly he turned and yanked my wrist again, forcing me to follow him up the stairs. His hold was so tight I was helpless against his strength.

"Alex, that's enough. Let go," I commanded. I also suddenly remembered Lilly's work schedule. I was alone with him.

I frantically started kicking and swinging my arms. Alex would never hurt me...would he? He pinned both my arms behind my back, and pushed me a few yards to a room I assumed was his.

Jasper had warned me. I thought he was telling me to stay away from his cousin because of jealousy or something, and I only halfway believed him about Alex being an actual sociopath. Sure he made bad decisions, but I didn't think he was capable of something terrible.

"Let go!" I screamed. I started to yell something else, hoping that the neighbors would hear me, but Alex shoved me through the door—hard.

I slammed into a dresser. Pain erupted in my side. I tumbled to the floor, clutching the spot I hit.

"Why do you have to make everything so difficult?" Alex roared, raising the hairs on the back of me neck.

I brought myself to my feet, assessing my best route of escape. There was a window to my left, but we were on the second floor, and there was no overhang like there was outside my own window.

I had to find a way to get around Alex and escape through the door. I backed up, putting distance between us. He was so drunk; how quick on his feet could he possibly be?

Alex came closer, moving away from the door. I swallowed, my heart pounding in my head.

Alex was saying something, but his words were so jumbled up and angry that I couldn't decipher them. He lunged at me, but I was ready.

I sidestepped, making a quick dash for the door. Alex stumbled and fell to the floor.

He was too close to me. I felt a hand circle my ankle, causing me to trip. I screamed and attempted to kick my way free.

Alex stood and pulled me up by my waist, then slammed me against the wall. When my head took most of the impact, my vision blurred.

"Why are you doing this?" I managed, fighting back tears.

"What does it matter? Oportet sucks. The Outside sucks. Life just sucks, Luna."

He pinned me against the wall with his entire body. I tried one last time to fight against him, but his weight too much for me to get free. His eyes were crazed.

"Why aren't you into this? Why are you fighting?" The stench of alcohol coming from his hot breath against my face threatened my gag reflexes.

I was fighting because I didn't need the rules to tell me that this was wrong. Oportet didn't allow for its citizens to make their own choices, but I knew what I would choose—regardless of any written law. I would choose not to hurt people. That was the right choice. Alex was choosing wrong, and he was choosing it every single time.

Alex smashed his lips to mine. I kept my eyes wide open, pushing with all my strength to get him off of me. I refused to kiss him back.

I felt a tear escape my eye as I gathered every ounce of strength I had, channeling it all in an effort to stop the assault. Alex finally pulled his lips off mine and I used that opportunity to scream as loud as my vocal chords would allow.

Alex's large hand clamped over my mouth, releasing one of my arms. I slammed it into his chest, but he didn't move an inch.

I felt myself spiraling out of control, becoming hysterical. Tears streamed down my cheeks.

"Why the hell are you crying?" Alex muttered, and I thought I saw a glimpse of something besides lust creep into his eyes, maybe even remorse. It was gone as fast as it came, though, leaving me to understand just how far beyond repair he really was.

I had almost given up hope when I heard the faint echo of footsteps down the hall. Had Alex heard it to? Was he honestly thinking he was going to get away with this?

"As much as I love the dress, I bet you would look even better without it," he slurred.

That was when the most violent thought I'd ever had sprung into my consciousness: I wanted to kill him. I wanted to see Alex fall to the ground and never move again. I wanted his eyes to be void of life, his limbs motionless pieces of flesh and bone. I closed my eyes.

Alex's crooked smile vanished as the sound of footsteps reappeared.

"Fuck," he muttered. He glared into my eyes, his raw, evil anger sending the coldest of chills down my spine. "If you make any sound at all, I swear to God I will cut out your tongue."

I believed him.

I used my free hand to slam it against the wall, and the noise seemed like the loudest thing I had ever heard.

In a split second two things happened at once: Alex's door flew open, and Alex released me, only to spin me around and send me flying towards the dresser.

I was lucky the first time when I hit my side. This time, my head collided with the edge of the wood.

I was spinning. I tried desperately to stop—the motion creating a kind of nausea I had never experienced before—but there I was, spinning and spinning until the room came in and out of focus, until darkness pushed its way toward me, enveloping me into its numb embrace.

~~~~~

My head hurt. Something like a blanket was on top of me, and I felt the plushness of a mattress beneath me. Where was I? How did I get there?

I opened my eyes to a room painted in dark blue, the window next to the bed casting daylight onto the carpeted floor. I noticed a backpack leaning against what I assumed was a closet door, and it only took me seconds to recognize the plain black design.

Everything came back to me in that moment. I knew where I was, I knew how I had gotten there, and I knew why I felt so terrible.

Alex had forced himself on me. Jasper had saved me.

I pushed myself up and out of bed—Jasper's bed. The sudden movement made me sway on my feet, still dizzy. I crept toward the closed door. I heard voices on the other side of the door, and I froze in place, my heart pounding and limbs heavy. I raised my hand, perplexed as I watched it begin to violently shake.

I placed my head against the cool wood, tuning into the voices.

"You did what?" I recognized the strained voice as Lilly's.

"We already gave him enough chances, and each time you let him charm you into believing he had somehow changed. He obviously hasn't," Jasper spat. The hatred in his voice sent a chill down the length of my spine.

"What are you saying, Jasper? That this is my fault?"

"No, of course not. I've covered for him for far too long, and this has just made the decision that much easier for me."

"So that's it? You didn't even think to come to me first?"

Jasper started to say something but Lilly cut him off.

"You just turned him in, and they made the decision on the spot?"

"He was already on probation. He was obviously drunk, and I made a point of explaining my concern for his violent tendencies." Jasper spat the words with an intense kind of rage. "The guards are holding him until you have a formal meeting with the Council. They need to make sure that we hold a different set of values, and then Alex will be taken back to the Outside."

"I don't know about this..."

"Mom, he would have... If I hadn't stopped him..." Jasper trailed off, and I had a pretty good idea of the horrible things we were both imagining.

"Neither of us knows exactly what happened," Lilly said, exasperated.

"Why are you defending him?" Jasper roared. There was a beat of silence, and when he spoke next his voice was more leveled. "What the hell is wrong with him?"

"You know what's wrong with him. Darren gave him enough bruises and blows to the head to really screw him up." The hallway was silent for a moment. "I need some space to wrap my head around this. You should go check on Luna."

I got back under the covers of the bed, feeling cold and empty inside. I counted each footstep as Jasper drew nearer to his bedroom door, the task somehow keeping me from falling apart.

Jasper slipped into the room, clicking the door shut behind him as quietly as humanly possible. When he turned and saw that I was sitting up, he just stopped and stared at me.

"Are you okay?"

"No."

"How's your head?"

"It hurts." There was no blood, but I could feel a lump the size of a ping-pong ball on the side of my temple where I hit it.

Jasper started moving again, making his way to the bed. He sat next to me, and rubbed his eyes.

"I'm so sorry, Luna," he murmured. He slowly raised a hand to my face, brushing across my cheekbone. "What happened?"

I swallowed, looking down at my hands. Jasper watched me, wrapping his fingers around mine.

I sighed. "I thought you would be home," I started, watching Jasper tense up. "He was drunk, and he just...wouldn't listen to me. I couldn't get away." I could almost feel the anger Jasper was sending off. "He pinned me against the wall, and then he kind of...kissed me." Jasper looked away, flinching like I had hit him. "He told me not to make any noise when he heard you in the house, but I did. Then I hit the dresser."

I looked down at my hands in his, my eyes widening as I took in the swollen, red nature of his knuckles. There was a layer of dried blood, and the thought of Jasper hitting something hard enough to cause that sort of damage made me uneasy.

"What did you do to your hand?"

"What do you think?"

I nodded, remembering how hard Jasper had hit Kevin. Even then I didn't remember his hand looking that bad.

"I beat the shit out of him."

"So he's being expelled from Oportet?"

"Yes."

Everything was still. Everything was quiet.

"I don't want to go home," I whispered.

"Then don't."

~~~~~

My parents had no idea that Jenna and I had ended our friendship. They happily allowed me to stay the night at her house. If they knew where I would really be spending the night then I would never be allowed to leave the house again, and Jasper would probably be expelled along with his cousin.

"I'll sleep on the couch," Jasper whispered into my ear. We had been talking and watching whatever movies I wanted until late into the night.

With Jasper it was easy to forget. He was like a drug that could take away all of the pain; and I was addicted.

"Lilly is okay with this?"

"Yeah, she doesn't care."

It was so unusual for me to hear about Lilly's laidback style of parenting. I knew my mother and father were at the far end of the parenting spectrum, but so was Lilly—in the opposite direction.

"Luna," Jasper whispered, barely audible. My head was resting on his shoulder, and Jasper was tracing designs into the palm of my hand. "I'm in love with you."

I had so many words forming in my mouth, but they were all trapped. The silence was so heavy, and all I could focus on was the feeling of Jasper's shoulders moving with each breath he took.

"And I'm in love with you," I said.

I had never felt closer to anyone in my entire life. To find someone that I would do anything, go anywhere, or even fight for was incredible.

In that moment, I knew that Jasper Williams could break my heart—and that I could break his.

Chapter Nineteen

....

When I opened my eyes, Jasper was staring at me in such a pained way. I had to take a moment to make sense of everything I had just remembered. "What's wrong?" I asked, not understanding his troubled expression.

"What did you remember?"

"I asked you first."

"You were crying, Luna."

I drew my brows together. I raised a hand to my face, feeling the moisture on my cheeks.

"What did you remember?" Jasper asked impatiently.

"Exactly what you didn't want me to." Everything made sense now. I knew there was something Jasper wasn't telling me—something he didn't want me to remember. And this was it. He didn't want me to remember everything not because of anything he did, but because he was trying to protect me from what his cousin did. "Alex," was all I said.

"I'm sorry... Again."

"Hey," I said, grabbing his hand that rested between us. "Alex's actions were not your fault." I stared into his slightly panicked eyes, but almost immediately, his pained expression hardened. He looked away and pulled his hand from mine.

I had noticed the physical differences between Jasper from last year and Jasper from the present, but I was just coming around to distinguishing the emotional differences.

Jasper had all of his defenses up. He was closed off, and the walls he was using to defend himself were effectively keeping me at a distance. I didn't blame him. I wouldn't trust me either.

"Do you want me to take you home?" Jasper asked.

"Is that what you want?" Everything was becoming so confusing. One minute I thought we had a chance to pick up where we left off, and the next it felt like something was blocking that from ever happening.

"I'm leaving soon, Luna. I don't want you to become attached to something with an expiration date." Jasper spoke as if he was at a business meeting, his emotionless state slowly killing me inside.

"What are you saying?" This wasn't how it was supposed to end.

"I think that a clean break would be the most... beneficial... for both of us."

Anger boiled inside me. Jasper couldn't even look me in the eyes.

I had my answer. There was no hope for us. If there was, then Jasper would have put up more of a fight. Maybe he had nothing to fight for.

"I just don't get it. You keep contradicting yourself... It's like there's two different versions of you, and I never know which one will be making an appearance." When he came in through my window Friday night, it seemed like all he wanted was everything to return to how it was. Now he wanted to end it for good? It didn't add up.

"I know. You're just going to have to trust me on this, okay? I'm trying to do the right thing here. Please don't make this any more difficult than it already is."

I was far too angry to shoot back any of the coherent arguments swirling around in my brain, so I just pushed open the car door.

"Luna," Jasper started, putting his hand on my arm.

"Don't talk to me, and definitely don't touch me," I said, pulling my arm free and getting out of the car.

I tuned out whatever Jasper was saying behind me as I made my way to the forest, where his car couldn't trail me on the way back. There was no way in hell I was going to let him drive me home. I didn't even care that it was starting to pour down rain.

I learned the path to my house through my memories, and I tried without success to calm myself down as I navigated through the huge trees. I hated myself for thinking that Jasper would follow me into the forest, that he would tell me that he made a mistake.

Jasper was probably in his warm home right now, on his high horse believing his delusions about doing the right thing, while I was out in the rain loathing myself for believing my delusions about everything working out perfectly.

Since when had *anything* worked out perfectly? Last year we were hit with nothing but obstacles, but I still had hope that Jasper and I would have some sort of unrealistically flawless future together. I knew just how much that hopeful fantasy worked out. Someone took it all away, making any possible future with Jasper impossible.

It was a maddening cycle of hope and loss. Now all of my hope was gone, and the very thing that made me believe in the concept of hope was gone along with it.

I was alone, and it was all too easy for me to give up now that I had lost what I was fighting for.

~~~~~

I tried to keep myself busy until my parents returned from the conference. If I allowed myself any free time I'd surely suffer a mental breakdown.

The phone didn't ring. There was never a knock at the door. No one was climbing through my window.

Jasper wasn't bluffing. He was gone.

~~~~~

"How was your weekend with Stacy?" Mother asked Megan. My parents got home late last night, and they both seemed tenser than usual.

"It was great," Megan lied.

"What about you, Luna?" Father asked. "How big of a party did you throw?"

I smiled, finding legitimate humor in his joke. I might not have thrown a party, but I definitely hadn't played the perfect daughter role while they were gone. That smile quickly dissolved as the memory of Jasper cutting me out of his life replaced the memory of him kissing me in my bedroom.

"It was also great," I lied. The Beckham sisters had a pretty shitty weekend between the two of us.

"So, what was the big government thingy that brought everyone to the Capitol building?" Megan asked not-so-eloquently.

Mother cast a glance at Father before answering. "Well, this is a very confidential matter, and will not be released to the public for another couple weeks." Megan put on her best pout, her eyes pleading for details.

Normally, I would be begging right along with her, but I was having a hard time caring. I stared down at my plate of waffles, mindlessly moving pieces around with my fork.

"Okay, fine. You are forbidden to discuss this with anyone, do you understand?"

"Yes," Megan said with obvious excitement.

"Luna?"

I lifted up my head, momentarily puzzled by all the eyes at the table on me.

"What? Oh, sure, I won't say anything to anyone." Who would I tell?

"The Council has been drafting this plan for over a year now, and it was recently voted on and validated. The conference was to present this plan to all of the committees, my treasury committee included, and to set the plan into action. They're calling it the Expansion Project. I think the name is self-explanatory enough, isn't it?" Mother said icily.

"Um, no. What does that mean?" Megan asked, practically bouncing up and down in her seat.

"It means that I have to slave over paperwork for the next couple months, just to allocate funds for a project that puts my family in danger."

"Puts everyone in danger," Father added.

Megan and I exchanged annoyed looks at their lack of explanation.

"They're expanding Oportet," he elaborated.

"What? How?" I asked incredulously. They had my full attention now.

Mother's lips were tightened into a thin line. "Who knows? I'm not on a construction or defense committee, and the Council refuses to answer anyone's questions."

Father shot her a look, as if he was wordlessly chastising her tone when speaking of our leaders.

"They will be holding another summit this weekend to explain everything to everyone involved in the project. Your father has applied to be a part of the Defense Committee, to make sure our guards will be protecting Oportet the best they can."

Mother's lack of trust in our government was surprising. She usually put her absolute faith in the Council and all of its decisions. It was against Rule Number Two to do anything else.

Father cleared his throat. "That's enough about that, let's talk about how your school year has been going, Megan. You're about halfway through the semester, aren't you?"

The conversation was officially over, leaving me to drown in my own thoughts. At least now I had others to dwell on besides Jasper, like the mental image of Oportet's walls being torn down.

I had to admit, I almost liked the thought of everything that separated us from the Outside reduced to crumbled ruins.

I wished I had been born on the Outside. That would have made my life so much simpler. I wouldn't have had to suppress all of the thoughts that weren't up to par with this society's values, everything I said and did would be free from restrictions, and I would have had the whole truth from the start.

There was a small part of me that wished my memories had stayed buried. Ignorance was bliss, and what had I gained from knowing the truth? Jasper didn't want me anymore, Aunt May was dead, and I was trapped playing the part of a brain-wiped version of myself—while I was actually dying inside from all that I knew and not being able to do anything about it.

Was I really better off?

Chapter Twenty

....

Winter break came and went, and spring was steadily approaching. My life was made up of time spent at Aunt May's home, time spent with Jasper and Lilly, and the lull of schoolwork and family time.

As the year progressed, my parents were pestering me more and more about what I planned to do during my gap year—and what I planned to do with my life.

Jasper and I rarely spoke about the future. We figured that if we didn't talk about it, then it wouldn't come. All we could hope for was for everything to stay as it was.

I finished my sessions with the school counselor. I had been meeting with her every Wednesday, and by the end I had her totally convinced that she had changed me, that I was a model citizen again, and that what I had said about being brainwashed was just something Jasper had led me to believe.

I was sitting at my desk, working on a research paper for English class. I complained with everyone else when it was first assigned, but I was secretly looking forward to having the excuse to write. I just wished I could write about something other than the mechanics of Oportet's government.

I had my headphones in, listening to a disk Jasper had given me for my birthday. It was filled with my favorite music from the Outside.

My parents both had laptops of their own that they used for work, and they had bought a family laptop years ago so that Megan and I could work on school assignments.

Jasper had shown me how to play music from the disk without burning the files to the computer, which meant I could listen without leaving a trace. I shuddered at the thought of my parents listening to the music on this CD—the music that evoked emotion, rather than the dull music allowed in Oportet.

I had the volume turned up far too high, so when I felt a hand on my shoulder it scared me half to death. I ripped the headphones from my ears and spun around in my desk chair, only to meet Jasper's eyes. I opened my mouth and then closed it. How was he in my room?

"Remember when I bet you I could climb the drainage pipe, pull myself onto the overhang, and get in through your window?"

My jaw dropped. I almost didn't believe what he was implying.

"Well, when you just laughed at me, you were basically creating a challenge. Consider that challenge accepted... and completed.

"That's insane. You could have fallen and broken your neck!"

Jasper just grinned, and I knew that I wasn't being taken seriously.

"Wow. I guess you weren't lying about working on that essay," Jasper said, looking over my shoulder. I shut the laptop. "Overachiever. Isn't that thing due in two weeks?"

"Yeah, but I actually like writing, remember?"

Jasper just rolled his eyes. "I didn't think you liked it that much."

"We only get so many writing assignments, and it's against the rules to write about anything interesting on my own, so what else do I have?" I shrugged. If what I really wanted to do was off-limits, I at least had this.

"I have an idea," Jasper said like he was talking to a child, looking at me as if there was something obvious I was missing. "Why don't you write in a journal? You could write whatever you wanted, and all you would have to do is hide it somewhere. No one would ever read it except for you."

I had considered a similar idea a while back, but I had been too concerned about the rule-breaking aspect. Things were different now, and the excitement of being able to act on my desires to write creatively was growing.

"I think I'll do that."

Jasper looked pleased with himself. "I've been told that I'm an excellent problem solver."

"Humble, too," I joked.

I was feeling a sudden sense of paranoia at the single door that separated all that I had worked to hide from my parents. Thinking about what would happen if they saw Jasper in my room was enough to evoke a wave of nervous nausea.

It all disappeared when I remembered that they were working late. I also remembered telling Jasper this, which explained his calm demeanor. I doubt he would have risked anything if my parents had been home. He was on probation, after all.

"What do you want to do?" I asked. "With your life, I mean."

Jasper was lounging on my bed, his hands behind his head. He had no problem with making himself at home anywhere he was.

"I don't know," was all he said.

"You seem to really like music," I hinted. Surely there was something Jasper was passionate about.

"But what does that matter? I can't make a job out of that here."

I stayed quiet, confused by the sudden anger in Jasper's voice.

"I used to play a bunch of instruments, you know. My dad taught me," he continued.

I swallowed. Jasper usually avoided talking about his father.

"Piano, guitar, drums...they were all my escape."

Why didn't I know this? I was feeling hurt thinking about how much I had opened up to Jasper, when there was still so much he was keeping closed off.

"Dad was in a band until I was born. He wanted to settle down for me. That didn't stop him from passing on all of his musical expertise, living vicariously through me. It wasn't like I didn't share his love for music, though—because I did. I really did."

Now that Jasper was telling me these things I had this nagging fear that he would close up again. I needed him to keep talking.

"When he died, it all stopped. When I sat down to write a song, nothing came. I couldn't even touch an instrument without feeling like he was dying all over again." Jasper paused to take a deep breath. "My dad was the reason I got into music in the first place. When he died, it seemed wrong that my music got to keep on living. Now I don't even have a choice in the matter. I wouldn't be able to start playing or writing again if I wanted to." Jasper suddenly sat up, meeting my eyes. "I'm sorry, I didn't mean to—"

"Don't apologize. I'm glad you're letting it all out. I know how much it sucks to have your thoughts attacking you—and never doing anything but keeping them trapped inside."

"Sometimes I wish we had never moved to Oportet."

Ouch.

"But then I remind myself that I would never have met you."

Okay, that was better.

"I even avoided listening to music after he was shot, Luna. The first time I got into my mom's smuggled CDs was after I met you. I started to love music again because of you. I used to feel guilty, but I think I've finally come to understand that it's what my dad would have wanted. That's all I really care about."

"You're right. I think your dad would want you to be happy. Music obviously does that."

"It isn't the only thing that makes me happy," Jasper said, relief flooding through me at the sight of his mouth forming one of his patented mischievous grins.

I smiled back, crawling into his lap. Jasper wrapped his arms around me, holding me against him. My heart was fluttering in my chest, stopping altogether when he leaned down and brushed his lips against my neck.

"You changed everything," he whispered next to my ear. His breath feathered along my neck, making my skin tingle.

I had always known how much my life had changed since meeting—and subsequently falling in love with—Jasper, but I had never really considered how I had impacted his life.

What Jasper said about music made a lot of sense. Falling in love was like the perfect song. It filled you with all of these powerful emotions, made you forget how to breathe, lifted you up and tore you apart, left you speechless and so full of words all at once.

~~~~~

I had been thinking a lot lately about my childhood. Looking back now, I saw everything so much differently: the books we read, the papers we wrote, and everything we were taught to accept.

One of my fifth-grade teachers had always stuck out as the scariest and strictest in my elementary school. Her students cowered to her every whim to avoid her wrath, which simmered just below the surface, ready to erupt at the slightest infraction. She was the teacher that assigned an essay on the meaning of life.

As my peers frantically searched their class notes and dug through their memories to construct the perfect response, I was frowning in my seat. I knew the answer she was looking for. It was something that had always haunted me, something I understood from a young age. My parents drilled this answer into my brain until I no longer had to think about it.

The meaning of life was not supposed to be a deep, subjective, or provocative question. It should not have been a hard question for an elementary student in Oportet. I remember staring at a blank sheet of paper for hours at my little desk in the living room, a crease growing on my forehead as I thought.

The problem was not that I couldn't think of anything to write. The problem was that I didn't want to write it. I felt bothered, restricted, and even a little saddened. Mother eventually sat next to me on the floor, looking up at me worriedly.

"What's wrong, Luna? You know what to write," she cooed, almost like she was trying to coax the words out of me.

"Why?"

Mother's face hardened at the defiant tone in my voice. "Why what?"

"The answer is to follow the rules, trust the Council, go to school and apply for a useful job, and then retire at age sixty-five. The meaning of life is to live with a clear and set purpose," I said slowly, wracking my brain for anything I was missing. We had taken notes a week earlier to help us prepare for the paper that would comprise a huge portion of our grade. "But why?"

"If you don't do those things, then your life becomes meaningless. You become like an Outsider."

I nodded, trying to convince my mind to just shut down and listen to my mother. I didn't want to get into trouble.

"Outsiders hurt innocent people, lie to each other, run wild on the streets, and die having lived a worthless life. That's why we live here, and not out there. Following the rules, trusting your leaders, obeying your parents, and yes, eventually getting a job, are all a part of the perfect plan Oportet was founded upon. *Living your life according to this plan is really the only sensible way to live.*"

So that was what I wrote. I did not question the assignment further. What my mother said made perfect sense, and that was what I convinced myself to believe.

~~~~~

"If you think about it, calling anyone who doesn't live in Oportet 'Outsiders' is actually quite brilliant," Aunt May said, setting her tea down on her coffee table.

I loved talking with May. We had the most intelligent—and oftentimes beautiful—discussions about life.

"Training those included within a society to regard those outside of it like they are a completely different species encourages a sense of superiority. It encourages a dualistic mindset. It's us versus them. Good versus evil. Those living the right way pitted against those living the wrong way."

I nodded. Hearing Aunt May speak was like trying to decipher a genius's language. It took me a moment to wrap my brain around her complex ideas. After I came to understand her point, though, it was like a huge piece of the puzzle was set in place. What she said made a profound level of sense, and I could feel the truth of her words already within me. I just never knew how to express them.

"So when are you going to introduce me to this boyfriend of yours?"

I could feel my cheeks reddening, and I smiled at the thought of my two favorite people meeting. There was not even a possibility that May and Jasper wouldn't get along. They were already so similar.

"Soon. I promise," I said. I meant it, too.

May's phone began to ring. She held up a finger to let me know it would only take a second. She bounced over to the phone, tucking her gorgeous blonde hair behind her ear. Something about her demeanor changed as she began talking, her voice lowering until I could no longer make out her words. I pretended I wasn't paying attention as she cast a glance my way.

I had noticed this same behavior during other phone conversations I had witnessed. May seemed to be keeping whoever was on the other line, and whatever they were discussing, a secret. I was dying to know the truth.

May mouthed "sorry" to me before stepping into a different room, closing the door behind her. She wasn't even trying to be subtle anymore.

I tapped my foot against the carpet, internally debating whether or not to do something incredibly selfish and rude. I took in a deep breath, coming to a decision.

Life was too short.

I tiptoed to the closed door, pressing my ear against the cool wood. Eavesdropping had become a nasty habit for me lately. Why did everyone have to be so secretive anyway? Once my curiosity was provoked, there was no stopping it from making me do incredibly thoughtless things.

"When?" I heard Aunt May ask the mysterious person on the other side of the line. "That soon?"

She sounded panicked.

"I know, I know. Are you sure he will follow through? We don't need any slip-ups with his part of the plan. It could cost us everything."

There was a long pause, and my heart made a jump when I realized that Aunt May might have already ended the conversation. She could open the door at any second to find her niece on the other side of the door, completely disregarding her privacy.

The funny thing about guilt was that it always kicked in just after the crime was committed, but never during.

Before I could move, May spoke again. "I really do. I want the best for her, and I feel like I would be abandoning her. I promised myself that I would make sure she had a chance. I always knew she was special."

I gulped, a shiver running down my spine. She was referring to me. The way she spoke of "her" was making me want to cry. Aunt May loved and appreciated me for who I truly was, not what I pretended to be. That was all I ever wanted from my family.

What did she mean when she spoke of abandoning me? Did she decide that meeting with me was the wrong thing to do? This had always been one of my deepest fears, but I had always written it off as being a ridiculous insecurity. Aunt May enjoyed being in my life just as much as I enjoyed being in hers, right?

"I know. Trust me, I know. We'll talk soon, okay? I have to go," May said softly, her voice shaking slightly. "Love you, too."

My eyes widened. Was Aunt May in some sort of secret relationship? Why would she keep that from me?

In a daze, I felt the blood drain from my face at the sound of her footsteps. I had to go. Now.

Walking lightly on the balls of my feet, I made my way back to the peach-colored chair next to the coffee table. I felt my body hit the chair just as May stepped out from her room, and I could tell that it was taking more effort than usual for her to put a smile onto her angelic face.

"Sorry about that," she said, placing the phone on her kitchen counter and running a hand through her hair.

"It's fine," I said, trying just as hard to not sound phased by what I had just overheard, or out of breath from darting back to my seat.

"So what were we talking about?" Before I could even open my mouth she started speaking again, and the normal Aunt May resurfaced—never missing a beat. "Ah, yes. We were talking about Jasper," she said with raised eyebrows and a playful grin.

~~~~~

"I'm done with this," Jasper said. We were sitting in the forest, bundled up in warm clothing to beat the thirty-degree wind chill. Spring had decided to postpone its arrival this year by throwing us another round of freezing temperatures.

"With what?"

Jasper and I almost never fought. Aunt May had seemed skeptical when I told her this, claiming that every healthy relationship had conflict. I just shook my head and smiled. We were both so alike—cleverly avoiding confrontation and making sure we were considerate of each other's feelings—which made fighting a rare occurrence. Every fight we ever had ended in either laughing or kissing, sometimes both.

"With all of this."

I had already picked up on the fact that Jasper was in a pissy mood, so I was trying my best not to add to it. His unusually pessimistic attitude and complaining was making that hard, and it was starting to bring me down with him.

I wanted to elbow him in the side and make him snap out of it. We could've been having a much better time.

I fought the urge to roll my eyes. "You'll have to be a little more specific," I snapped, unable to contain my annoyance.

Jasper picked up on it and glanced over at me, but his scowl only deepened. "I've been thinking," he started.

I waited, and maybe it had to do with whatever he was about to tell me, or maybe Jasper's negative energy was somehow transferring over to me, but my mood was rapidly turning sour.

"I think we should leave," he finished.

"What do you mean?"

"We should leave Oportet."

Shock flooded my system. Jasper's fight with Lilly must have truly been terrible if this was where his mind was now.

"Look, I know that you're in a mood, and that something happened between you and your mother, but I really don't think you're thinking clearly. We can't just leave."

"Why not?" Jasper asked defiantly, as if he was just begging for an argument.

"Because we have families, Jasper. Things might be bad in Oportet, but they aren't that bad. We can figure it out together, okay?"

"That's not good enough."

"Excuse me?"

Jasper shook his head. "You know that's not what I mea—"

"A life with me isn't good enough for you now?" I got up, brushing off pine needles and leaves from my pants after sitting on the bare forest floor. I knew what Jasper meant, but he was also making me angry, so I didn't feel like giving him that satisfaction.

"I don't understand why you don't want to go," Jasper said, jumping to his feet. "You don't agree with anything about Oportet, or your parents for that matter. What's keeping you here?"

I thought about the house that I had lived in my entire life, every memory ever made from within Oportet's walls, every smile, and every glimpse of joy. This was my home.

I then thought about Aunt May and Megan. I crossed my arms stubbornly.

"I might not agree with them, but I still love my family. It would crush them if I left."

"Is it really worth your happiness, though?"

"Who says leaving Oportet would make me happy?" Why didn't just being with me make Jasper happy?

"Oh, don't give me that. You've talked about it before. I know it's what you want."

"I guess you don't know me as well as you thought," I said before turning on my heel and storming off. I didn't want to talk about this anymore.

I stumbled over a rock jutting out of the ground, feeling a set of hands steadying me. I hadn't even heard Jasper behind me. I sucked in a breath, internally cursing my clumsiness. I shrugged out of Jasper's grasp, and started off again through the maze of trees.

"Luna."

I kept walking. What gave Jasper the right to tell me how to feel? Running off with him just because he was fighting with his mother was ridiculous. I couldn't leave Oportet. It wasn't even an option.

"Luna, wait."

I crossed my arms and faced him. My abrupt turn made him draw back. He met my glare with eyes drained by exhaustion.

"What?" In my head the word was sharper, stronger even, but the attempt was lost in Jasper's deflated disposition. My anger began to crumble, and for a moment I lost track of what we were even fighting about.

"Any life with you is more than enough."

Chapter Twenty-One

....

"Luna?"

The memory faded, and I started to see the real world again, flinching at the sight of a hand waving violently in front of my face. Megan was staring at me with raised eyebrows, a slight smile forming at the sight of my deer-in-headlights expression.

Where am I? I wondered.

I peered around, still lost in the past's intoxicating abyss. I was in the living room, lying back in a recliner. I was losing the ability to distinguish between the past and present. I was living two different lives, and one was infinitely more appealing: the life that no longer existed.

The past did not matter. My memories were the equivalent of a hopeless daydream. Life was never anything but *present*. Yet, here I was, clinging to my memories as if they were all that defined me.

"Luna? Are you okay?" Megan asked. Her smile faltered as she watched me.

"Yeah. I'm fine," I said, clearing my throat when my voice came out raspy and rough.

"Where do you go, Luna?" Megan asked quietly, glancing behind her to make sure we were alone. "And when you go there, what do you see?"

I looked at my sister in shock. *How did she know?*

I knew that I'd been zoning out a lot lately, fragments of memories coming to me at all times of the day. Almost anything triggered them now: a word, a thought, a voice, and sometimes even my own desires. I wondered how long it would be before someone would figure it out. How many memories would Tomlinson take away the second time? And would he take the pain away with them?

"You're doing it again."

"Sorry," I mumbled. "Just thinking about the future."

"I have a different theory."

My heart sped up. There was no way Megan could know— I'd been too careful.

"And what would that be?"

"You remember," Megan said, her green eyes big and knowing.

I said nothing. I took a deep breath and nodded, the slight movement only visible if someone was looking for it. Megan smiled.

"I knew it," Megan squealed.

She quieted herself when I shot her a glare.

"When you really believe in something, I can see it in your eyes. It's like this silent gesture to coax the other person into believing right along with you. When you talked to me in my room, you didn't have that look in your eyes. You didn't believe a word you said. Then I started noticing that same dead look whenever you spoke to Mother about the future, or to Father about Oportet's *perfect* rules. And when you weren't lying to everyone, you were off in some other world. I remembered you asking about your memories a while ago, then never mentioning them again after I shut you down. Then it all made sense. You've been remembering things."

"I think I'm close to the end," I said, partially to myself.

"Wow. This is crazy," Megan breathed. "The procedure was supposed to take it all away. For good."

So the story of me falling down the porch steps *was* all a lie. It was some kind of medical procedure that robbed me of my past.

"This... procedure... I still don't understand why Tomlinson did it. Why was I such a threat?"

Megan furrowed her brows, squinting at me like I was talking in gibberish. "What are you talking about? Is that what you think happened?"

Now it was my turn to be confused. Why did Megan feel the need to keep up the charade? Was Tomlinson's threat really that frightening?

"Girls?" Father's voice sent us both into an abrupt silence. "Can you two come into the dining room? We have some news about the Expansion Project."

I was flustered that our conversation was cut short, but the Expansion Project was just interesting enough to hold my anger at bay.

Megan and I made our way to the dining room, surprised to find Mother visibly unnerved. She was leaning against the back of one of chairs, her arms crossed, and she was staring off into the distance.

We sat down, and I watched as Mother masked her emotions, cleared her throat, and straightened up in her chair.

"The expansion has already been taking place, and we didn't even know it," she said quietly. "The new outer wall was built in secret, and has been built for over a year. The final step is to simply take down the current wall, which is programmed to quite literally sink down into the ground on command."

"Then they'll have to uninstall the current electronic gate and reinstall it into the new wall," Father added. "After the initial wall is taken down, the first shift of guards and technicians will move in to start the process of reinstalling the gate. There will always be a shift of guards at the entrance to protect us and to continue the completion of this instillation."

"It will begin this Thursday," Mother said.

"Wait," I started. "I thought the whole point of the conference you just went to was to vote on and discuss the possibility of an expansion."

Mother pursed her lips and shot a glance at Father.

"We do not question the authority of the Council. They know what is best for our society," he said.

"But that isn't fair! They went behind our backs," I protested. I opened my mouth to say more, but I was shot down by a look from Father.

"Luna!" he snapped. "We do not question."

I swallowed down my words, taking a deep breath.

"I am a part of the Defense Committee to oversee the installation of the gate on the new wall, so I will be working many late nights the next few weeks. Luna, I need you to accept some responsibility during this time by helping out your mother and taking care of Megan," Father said.

I nodded.

"I'm thirteen years old," Megan muttered. "I don't need someone to take care of me."

"What has gotten in to you two? If you don't collect your-selves in the next few seconds, there *will* be consequences," Mother said, exasperated. "We do not question authority. We do not correct authority. We listen and do what we are told. As soon as we forget these things, tragedy and chaos will present itself."

Megan opened her mouth, and I rushed to stop her from making a mistake she would come to regret.

"Yes, ma'am," I said, sending a look toward Megan.

She shut her mouth and trapped her words in. She did not yet understand that nothing she said could ever affect people who were so blindly attached to Oportet's way of thinking. It was impossible.

"Megan, go get some studying done," Mother commanded. Megan turned on her heel and walked out of the room.

Mother turned to me. "Something came up. I won't be able to take you into work with me Monday, but Wednesday just opened up, so you can visit the Occupational Placement Office then."

"Do you think Tomlinson would be available to meet with me?" I asked. My parents exchanged glances.

"Possibly," Father said slowly. "For what purpose?"

"My future. I think I was a bit too hasty when I said I want-ed to be a teacher. I'm still open to other options," I lied.

Mother was eating up my words, teeming with excitement at what I was hinting. "I'm sure that can be arranged. You must have at least a handful of favors available from your service to Oportet," she said.

"I look forward to speaking with him."

Chapter Twenty-Two

························

"He'll be home any minute now," Lilly assured me. "You seem... stressed." Was it that obvious? Second trimester's finals were approaching, and teachers from my advanced classes were handing out essays and projects at a pace I couldn't keep up with.

"I am." I sighed, following her into the house.

"I could help you with that, if you wanted."

"With the stress?" I asked, confused. She nodded. "Um, okay."

Lilly smiled and led me into a room I had never been in before. It appeared to be a living room of sorts, but it was mostly empty. A potted plant sat next to the curtained windows, and the room itself radiated a relaxing energy. The walls were painted a soothing lavender color, and sunlight streamed through the curtains onto a lightly colored wooden floor. What appeared to be rolled up blankets sat in a corner.

"Grab a mat, dear," Lilly said, gesturing to the corner. She sat down on the floor on a mat that was already unrolled. Her long dark hair was kept out of her face by her trademark flowery headband.

I did as I was told and grabbed a mat, setting it down a couple feet to the left of Lilly's. I had no clue what was going on.

"Ready to de-stress?" Lilly asked.

I mimicked her crossed-legged position. "I think so," I laughed uncomfortably.

"Trust me, you'll love it."

"What exactly is 'it?'"

"Close your eyes," she said.

I glanced at her self-consciously, only to find that Lilly already had her eyes shut tight. I closed my eyes and waited.

"Now," she continued, "focus on taking deep breaths and clear your mind."

"Impossible," I muttered.

Lilly ignored me. "When a thought comes into your head, do not attempt to remove it. You need to focus on not creating new thoughts—and accepting the ones that pop up on their own. Do not dwell on them, and they will pass on. If it will help, you can also visualize a kind of filing cabinet within your mind. File away each of your worries into sections: family, school, and so on."

I took a deep breath. I felt silly, but if Lilly's peculiar de-stressing method really worked, then it wouldn't hurt to give it my best shot.

I started with school. I went through all of the assignments and tests I was worried about, and then mentally tucked them away. I then focused on my worries about the future: Jasper and his role in it, my future occupation, and my violent opposition of the Council's authoritarian rule. I got so caught up in my thoughts about the future that I completely forgot what I was doing.

I decided to move on, having filed away my stressors the best I could. I took in deep breaths, and tried to follow Lilly's instructions. I let thoughts pass through my mind, trying my best not to dwell on them and create more. It proved to be a difficult task.

Then, it all fell away. My mind was quieter at that moment than it had ever been, and I was determined to stay in that state for as long as I could.

Suddenly all of my worries seemed utterly ridiculous. Worrying about my future was keeping me from fully enjoying my life in the present. This revelation started to expand within me, and I felt like I was truly onto something... then I heard a quiet burst of laughter.

My eyes flew open to see Jasper leaning against the doorframe with a crooked grin on his face.

Lilly and I spoke at the same time, me saying, "shut up, Jasper," just as Lilly said, "Jasper, go away."

Jasper somehow found this to make the situation even more amusing, and he laughed all the way into a different room.

"Sorry about my little ass of a son," Lilly said, trying her hardest to hold back her own laughter.

I glanced over at her, and we both busted out laughing.

"How do you feel?"

"Better." I glanced at the clock that I noticed before, and looked back at Lilly incredulously. "An entire hour?"

"Crazy, isn't it?"

I stretched and returned my mat to the corner. "Thank you, Lilly."

"Next time I'll kick Jasper out of the house for the whole day." She winked, smiling warmly at me.

She closed her eyes again, and I shut the door behind me quietly as I left.

"Have a good meditation session?" Jasper struggled to keep a straight face, his infuriating smile leaking through each time his mouth opened.

I picked up a pillow from the couch beside me and chucked it at his head, and he raised an arm to deflect it. I crossed my arms and glared at him.

"You know, hippies are supposed to be non-violent."

I had no idea what a hippy was, but Jasper used it in a fairly derogatory manner, so I could only assume he was insulting me.

"You really are an ass."

Jasper grinned and moved toward me, bending down to kiss my forehead. My glare broke, and I cursed myself for letting my lips form a small grin. He had ruined my moment with Lilly; he did not deserve to make me smile.

"I need to show you something," Jasper said, taking my hand and leading me to the family room.

We sat down at the desk where his laptop sat, and I watched as Jasper slid a CD labeled "Jasper" into the slot. I glanced at his face, trying to read his expression. Was Jasper letting me listen to his music? He refused to meet my eyes as he navigated the computer screen.

"I thought I smashed them all after my dad died," Jasper said in a flat tone. "She hid one from me."

"Lilly?" I asked, receiving a nod from Jasper. I had no idea Jasper had tried to destroy his own music. "What made her decide to give it back to you?"

"She didn't think I'd smash it. Not now." Jasper finally looked at me. "She thought I might want to show it to you."

"Do you sing?" I asked. I thought of all the bands Jasper had introduced me to from the Outside. The lyrics were the best part of the songs, words weaving together emotions and thoughts so deeply connected to the artist's mind. How amazing it would be to take a peek into Jasper's.

"Sometimes." He pressed play.

~~~~~

"Luna? Luna, snap out of it!" Mother's voice jolted me to the present.

I shut my eyes, trying to hold on and listen to the melodic piano playing on Jasper's laptop.

"Luna!"

"Shut up!" I exploded. My eyes came into focus to see the stunned faces of my mother and sister staring back at me. Megan's mouth hung open, her fork dropping a glob of spaghetti back onto her plate. A vein in Mother's neck stuck out, her lips tightened into a straight line. Father was working late tonight, so it was just the three of us.

"Excuse me?" Mother asked.

"This is your fault!" I wanted to scream. "You let him do this to me!" I wanted to throw it in her face and watch her crumble. I wanted to explode, but no words came out. This was all because of Tomlinson and his manipulation, and I was all too done with my family acting like it was okay. They sat back and watched as my own mind was put into the shredder—tearing it apart until there was nothing left.

"I apologize," I finally mumbled. "I have a migraine."

Mother just looked at me for a few long seconds before getting up from the table, returning with a fat pain-reliever pill.

I took it from her palm. "Thank you. May I be excused?" The second Mother nodded her consent, I was standing and heading for the stairs.

I clicked the door shut behind me and collapsed on my bed. I stared up at the ceiling, calmly waiting for my memory to return.

It did.

~~~~~

"Beautiful," I said.

The piano was truly captivating, the melody fading in and out, speeding up and slowing down.

Then Jasper started to sing. His voice was smooth and resonating, the words somehow lost as I paid attention to the haunting melody. I looked over at him beside me, but he was staring out the window.

I focused on the lyrics: "I'm not lost, but I'm not sure where I am. You might see me, darling, but I'm not really there."

"This is amazing," I breathed. I smiled softly, trying to get Jasper to meet my eyes. He needed to know that I heard him—he might have been lost before, but he wasn't now. I could see him; he was really there.

"I sound like a stereotypical angst-y teenager. There's no substance," he muttered.

"Jasper. Listen to me," I begged. "Look at me." Jasper turned his head, searching my face like it could present him with the answers he needed. "Everyone feels lost, but that doesn't invalidate anything that you feel." Jasper remained silent. "This is seriously amazing. You're so talented."

The next song began to play, this one faster and more demanding. A bass guitar accompanied the keyboard in an intricate weaving of harmonies.

"This is what I was meant to do, Luna," Jasper finally said. "Can't you understand that?"

"Of course I can. I—"

"Then why is it so hard for you to understand that I can't stay here?" Jasper interrupted. "I can't stay in a place that suppresses who I am."

I could feel my heart shattering in my chest. It was a terrible, disturbing feeling. My chest felt like it was imploding—a tangible, physical ache. Jasper had to leave, but I needed to stay.

"How would you leave?"

"I'll ask the Council. They force people out all the time. If I wanted to leave, I don't see why they would stop me."

I remembered what May had told me about her friends that had made a similar request. They came back with their minds completely changed. May said it had been "a complete one-eighty." Whatever the Council had done to intimidate them, I doubted Jasper would be immune to that same power.

"When?" I asked. I was screaming at myself internally: Tell him! Warn him! Selfish, selfish, selfish!

"Come with me," Jasper pleaded. "I have arranged a meeting with them Friday."

"What?" I stood up. "Friday? Were you planning on sneaking away? Were you even going to tell me?"

"Of course I was, don't be ridiculous."

That was when I decided to commit the most selfish act against Jasper I could think of. I was going to let him fall into the Council's trap.

"You can tell me how the meeting goes Friday night."

~~~~~

Aunt May was acting more and more strange as time went on. The mysterious phone calls kept coming, and she was acting awfully sentimental. She kept asking me about the future, about Jasper, and about my journaling. I was in no mood to talk about the previous two topics, but I gladly discussed my newfound love for writing prose.

I told her that I would let her read some of my stories the next time I saw her, and my beautiful aunt started to cry.

"What's wrong?" I asked. A few fat tears rolled down her face, and I was so surprised that I struggled to know how to comfort her.

"Nothing, dear. I'm just really happy you're finally discovering who you are." May smiled, and I laughed nervously.

"Um... thanks."

Aunt May was keeping something huge from me, and I was desperate to figure out what it was.

"Sorry, I must sound crazy right now." May laughed, wiping the tears from her face.

"Yeah, a little," I said, keeping my tone joking. I glanced at the clock, standing up quickly when I realized the time. I told my parents I was staying after school for tutoring, and it was past time for when I was supposed to be home. "I have to go. Can we meet tomorrow at four?"

"Yes, but I have to be somewhere at five," Aunt May replied, her voice cracking.

She stood up and wrapped me in a hug. I was starting to feel extremely uncomfortable about all of these signs. What were they pointing to? What was I missing?

"I'll see you tomorrow," she whispered as she pulled away. She forced a smile—a smile so full of sorrow and regret, yet determination shining through the cracks. Aunt May was going through with whatever she was crying about, and nothing was going to change her mind.

Chapter Twenty-Three

Today is the day I will confront Councilman Tomlinson. Today is the day I will find out *why*.

"Luna? Are you ready to go?" Mother called from downstairs.

I slipped into a professional-looking navy skirt and tucked in my white blouse. I then slid my feet into terribly uncomfortable shoes that Mother all but forced me to wear. I could already feel blisters forming as I wobbled down the stairs, clutching the banister as I went.

"You look ridiculous," Mother said from the front door. I could tell she was holding back laughter, and I shot her a look of irritation.

"I told you I was bad with heels," I retorted.

"Go change. Wear some black flats or something."

I let out a breath of relief. "Thank God," I muttered. I unbuckled and stepped out of the shoes in a hurry.

"Thank who?" Mother asked, cocking her head. I thought about it for a moment, realizing that I had just repeated something I always heard Jasper say. I honestly had no clue who I was thanking.

"Um, never mind. I'll go change." I carried the heels up the stairs, a sinking feeling in my chest at the thought of Jasper.

~~~~~

I sat in Mother's office, my stomach churning as I ran through how I was to confront Tomlinson. The fear of wasting the opportunity when it finally presented itself weighed heavily on my mind. Did I really have the courage to go through with this? If I approached Oportet's leader, the man who, with the wave of a hand, had the power to wipe my entire mind, would I really be able to use my words the right way?

Mother was typing away on her computer, her face rigid. She rubbed her eyes, her limbs moving in slow motion when the phone began to ring.

She took her time raising the phone to her ear, and I straightened up in my chair. I took deep breaths as I waited.

"I'll send her down right away," Mother said, sending a nod my way. She gave me a small smile, but I was far too nervous to do anything but breathe.

It will all be okay, I told myself. I repeated the line in my head until it was nothing but a way to keep my mind distracted. I repeated it as I exited Mother's office, as I waited in the elevator, and as I steered through the hallways of the vast government building.

The walls were white. The floors were white. It even smelled like *white.*

The Council members and close advisers—like my Father— were located in an annex that was attached to the main building. Before I could pass through the connecting hallway, I would have to face the Council's relentless security system.

There were three armed guards positioned there now, and the one manning the electronic, steel doors leading to the Council's headquarters looked up as I approached. The other two were stationed at either side of the doors, their faces stone-like.

"Name?" the guard at the desk asked me.

"Luna Beckham." The attempt to make my voice sound strong and purposeful only half-worked, making me sound more like an intimidated teenager.

The guard typed something on the large, sleek computer at his desk—technology like I'd never seen before. The man gave me a slight nod before typing something else on his computer, followed by a loud mechanical noise emanating from the Council's building.

The steel doors glided open within seconds, and the two guards positioned in front of it moved to let me pass.

I took yet another deep breath and moved on through the doors. The connecting hallway was entirely concrete—and *dark*. The only light came from the flickering fluorescents positioned along the walls. At the end of the hallway was another set of guards, but only two this time.

In between the two guards was the large body scanner Father never stopped complaining about.

I could not help but feel awkward as I walked down the long hallway, the two guards focused on my approach. I suddenly had to concentrate to walk normally under their scrutiny. The sound of my feet hitting the concrete echoed dramatically against the walled enclosure.

"Step through," one of the guards said when I reached the end. When I stepped into the machine, the guard studied the screen on the other side. Finding nothing incriminating, he signaled for the second guard to type a code into the wall next to the doors.

"Have a nice day, Ms. Beckham," he said.

I did not have time to figure out how he knew my name before I was ushered through the second set of doors.

"Thanks," I mumbled as I passed.

I was finally inside the Council's main building. I took out the folded map from my pocket, studying the path marked in red that led to Tomlinson's office. The offices of the councilmen were located in the very center of the building.

I made my way down the first hallway, turning left at the end, and then took an elevator to reach the second floor. In the elevator, a man in the corner was speaking into what appeared to be a small wireless phone. I did not think that those kinds of devices were allowed in Oportet. I glanced at it out of the corner of my eye, worried that the man would notice me staring. He was too caught up in his conversation to pay any attention to me, though.

The technology I had observed in the Council's building and with the guards was far more advanced than the average citizen's possessions. What was so dangerous about these slim and sleek phones and computers?

The elevator came to a stop at the second floor. I exited, leaving the man and his intriguing technology behind. Moving through this final hallway I passed a woman with some kind of gadget attached to her ear. She was speaking like she was in the middle of a conversation. I looked around the hallway to see if I was missing something, but the hallway was empty. The earpiece must have been yet another kind of exotic communication technology.

When I reached Tomlinson's door, I paused a moment with my hand on the knob. *It will all be okay*, I repeated one final time.

I knocked three times and waited.

"Come in," said a voice from inside. I turned the knob and entered, my heart ramping up to a dangerous pace.

I shut the door behind me and took in my surroundings. The office was much larger and more luxurious than Mother's. Tomlinson sat at a large wooden desk, a full-sized bookshelf behind him. There was a leather couch to my left, leaning up against a red wall. I stood on an expensive looking carpet.

Tomlinson's face was withered by age and stress. "Sit, Luna," he instructed.

Something about the way Tomlinson commanded me brought all of my anger to the surface. The man who had caused me so much pain and confusion wanted me to sit before him and act calm and orderly, as if he hadn't destroyed my relationship with Jasper or ripped away my past.

The time for pretending had passed. It was time I received the truth I had been craving since I regained my first memory.

"No. I'm fine standing." Now I had his full attention.

Tomlinson studied my face, and a knowing smile reached his lips, like I was a petulant toddler who thought she had power over her parents.

"I can assume that you are not actually here to discuss your occupational decision, correct?" he asked.

The humor in his voice made me want to flip over his desk or break a lamp. It pushed me to throw the tantrum he obviously expected. It was because of this expectation that I managed to refrain.

"I want to ask you why you did what you did, and why you forced my family to lie to me about it. How did you manage to intimidate them into secrecy? Did you threaten them?"

Tomlinson leaned back in his chair, cocking his head to the side. "What is it that you think I did, exactly?" he said with a raised eyebrow.

"You forced me into a medical procedure to take away my memories, then you covered it up with the tale of a tragic *accident!*" I exclaimed.

I was expecting a lot of things from Tomlinson when I finally confronted him about what I knew—surprise, anger, and denial—but how he really reacted did not make the list.

Tomlinson laughed.

It was not the kind of sinister laugh of a man who was just caught in a crime and was powerful enough to get away with it; it was the laugh of a man who was just accused of a crime he was not responsible for.

This realization hit me hard. *Where had I gone wrong?*

"Is that what you think happened?" he asked when he was done laughing at me. I remembered a similar reaction from Megan earlier that week.

"Then what *did* happen?" I asked, my voice not as strong as it once was.

"You seem to be very emotional right now. I'm not sure that it would be wise to unload that kind of information." Tomlinson smiled, the same one he'd given at my OGS: a smile of *pity.* "Besides, it is not my place to say."

"I need to know," I said firmly. I had already uncovered most of the truth. There was no use hiding anything at that point.

"You should really ask your parents," Tomlinson said, and my stomach began to recoil against his words. "You really think a troubled adolescent is important enough for the Head

Councilman to concern himself with? How...egotistical. Don't get me wrong, your particular case has proven to be beneficial for me in the long run, but the choice to better your mind last spring had nothing to do with me, let alone the Council."

It felt like someone had knocked the air out of me. I couldn't remember how to breathe, how to speak, how to function. The answer had been right in front of me this entire time.

They were my family. How could they?

Time seemed to stop.

Soon I was out of Tomlinson's office, down the stairwell and through the connection hallway.

"Hey Luna!" Father called cheerfully, spotting me moving toward him in the hallway leading to the building's exit. "Everyone has been asking me how Bring Your Daughter to Work Day has been." He chuckled. "Imagine the look of envy your mother and I get when we explain that you're here to meet with Tomlinson," he gushed. As I came closer he began to scowl. "Is something wrong?"

"Don't you dare call me your daughter ever again," I said, moving past him toward the exit.

I pushed through the glass doors, the sunlight blinding me as I stepped outside.

~~~~~

It took me a little under an hour to walk home from the government building. I did not plan on staying there long, just long enough to force the truth out of my little sister and pack up my things.

The middle school let out at two-thirty, and it was around three now. Megan should've been home.

"Luna?" I heard Megan call from her room. "Is that you?"

I shut the front door behind me and made my way up the stairs. Megan's door was wide open, and she was sitting at her desk with an Algebra textbook open. She turned her head as I entered, looking at me with concern.

"Why are you home early? Did something happen?" Megan looked scared now, and I could only imagine the look on my face.

I wanted to cry out for the betrayal, lying, and scheming committed against me by my own family, but somehow I contained myself.

"It wasn't Tomlinson who erased my memories. It was Mother and Father," I said.

Megan's face paled. "Luna, they only wanted the best for you. They thought they were doing the right thing. I know now that it was wrong and terrible, and I hate myself for not speaking up, but they *really believe* in all of this. They wanted to fix you."

"I wasn't broken!" The urge to break something once again presented itself. "Tell me exactly what happened. *Now*."

"First you got into a fight, and you were sympathizing with the *Outsiders*. Next you were spending far too much time out of the house. It made them feel so powerless. They were losing control of you. They suspected you were still seeing him— Jasper." Megan's big green eyes let out a single tear, and she quickly wiped it with her sleeve.

"One night, you came home an absolute wreck. Right after that we found out Aunt May had died in a car wreck. You were talking all crazy, and Mother began to suspect you had been meeting with May, too." Megan paused, contemplating something. She shook her head like she had decided against it. "It was crazy talk," she repeated.

"It wasn't too long before Mother called in a favor at her office and had a device installed to tap into your phone calls. One night, she used it. I remember her completely losing it. She was screaming at Father about how they had to act quickly, or they would lose you forever."

"Because I wanted to leave," I whispered. It was all coming together now. The pieces were connecting. The puzzle was almost complete.

Megan nodded. "The next day a couple of guards showed up on our doorstep. You fought them, and that's when you fell and hit your head."

"Wait, I thought there was a medical procedure?" I asked, interrupting her.

She shot me a glare, letting me know that she was getting to that. "You hitting your head was truly an accident, and you didn't hit it hard enough to have amnesia. They took you away in a black van."

My head was spinning. I thought I wanted the truth, but the truth was too painful.

"Dr. Gary Reynolds was the neurosurgeon who carried out the procedure. I remember Mother inviting him over for dinner while you were resting in the hospital." Megan shook her head again, as if realizing how twisted that was. "You woke up, and everything was back to normal."

"Normal," I echoed quietly. The name of the neurosurgeon—Dr. Gary Reynolds—earned a nudge from within my mind. He was an important puzzle piece, I was sure, but where did he fit?

"What are you going to do, Luna?" Megan asked, fear lacing every word. "Please don't go."

"I can't stay in this house anymore."

"Please don't *go*."

I locked eyes with her, and a look of understanding passed between us. She was pleading with me to stay for the same reason I clung to Aunt May in my memories. I held the key to her freedom. Megan wanted me to free her mind. She was telling me that she was ready, just as I had been when I showed up on May's doorstep.

It was at that moment—the split second in which Aunt May crossed my mind—that my grip on the present moment began to diminish.

"Luna? Are you remembering something?"

Chapter Twenty-Four

··

I was furious at Jasper for arranging a meeting with the Council later that night, but I felt even guiltier for letting him walk into a trap. Aunt May warned me that the Council could manipulate people that wanted to leave Oportet into wanting to stay.

I told my parents that I was going for a bike ride. In reality, I was keeping my promise to visit my uncharacteristically emotional aunt.

I left my bike leaning against the garage door before climbing the front porch steps. I knocked three times and waited. Aunt May was on the phone when she swung the door open, and she didn't greet me before she stalked off in the other direction, furiously waving about the arm not holding the phone.

"It has to be right now. I just spoke to him, and he says we only have an hour before the window closes," May said. "Yes, I know, but it's not like medical paperwork is really going to matter after all of this is over." May paused again. "Look, Gary, I have to go. My niece is here."

I was waiting by the door, trying to decipher the meaning of May's peculiar conversation. May hung up the phone and turned to face me.

"I apologize for my rudeness," May said in an even, flat tone.

"Is everything okay?" I asked.

May paced back and forth. "Um, how about you stay here while I run an errand for a friend," she said finally.

"Okay," I mumbled.

May brushed past me in a hurry, swinging a black backpack over her shoulder. She placed a hand on the doorknob, only to hesitate and look back at me. Her eyes glowed, and her lips trembled.

"Luna?"

"Yes?"

May twisted the doorknob.

"Follow your gut instincts," she said. "I love you."

"I love you too," I said as she stepped through the door.

When the door fell shut, it was time to move. I peered through the curtains in the living room, watching as May got into her car and pulled out of the driveway. As soon as she started moving down the street, I flung open the front door and raced toward my bike.

The speed limit, as written in the rules, was twenty miles per hour in all residential areas. I pedaled furiously to keep May in sight. The periodic stop signs kept me in the chase, allowing me time to put myself close enough to see her car, but far back enough to stay undetected.

May turned left, moving further and further away from the main part of town. She was heading to the outskirts, to the city's border. In fact, she was heading straight for the main gate—the electronic entrance to Oportet manned by designated guards. It only opened a few times a year, to transport new citizens from the Outside.

I had little time to think as I trailed May's sleek, red vehicle through the winding neighborhood roads. Oportet was organized so that the government building was in the very center, and it was surrounded by the scientific and medical centers. The next layer was the schools and occupational training centers, and then the business and commercial sectors followed. The final layer was the residential area that surrounded the rest of the society. Beyond the rows of houses lay Oportet's walls.

The layout of the city revealed the Council's priorities and rankings of importance. If the wall was ever breached, the people would be the first to go, and the Council would be the last.

My muscles ached. I had already lost sight of May on multiple occasions. A series of lucky guesses kept me on her trail. My suspicion was proving to be accurate: May was heading for the exit.

I had never been so close to the walls before. They seemed to be made of a kind of metal, and they stood at least fifty feet tall. May slowed her car to a stop, parking it where the road ended and cutting the engine. There were no more houses beyond this road, just dirt and nothingness—then the wall. The houses lining this road looked completely abandoned, yards filled with weeds and overgrown grass, and broken or shattered windows.

Suddenly aware of the lack of cover, I spotted a crumbling brick mailbox. I pedaled over to the mailbox and dumped the bike. My legs, worn out from the frantic ride through town, screamed in protest as I crouched behind my brick hiding spot.

Aunt May exited the parked car. She turned right and disappeared behind the row of houses. I jogged to the end of the street, peering in the direction May had gone. She was moving along the dirt stretch of land next to the wall, getting closer and closer to the wall's lone opening.

I had to know where May was going. I had to know the reason behind all of the mysterious phone calls and cryptic goodbyes. I had to know why May was leaving me, and how she was planning on doing it. If she really was planning to walk through Oportet's gates, I needed to see her do it with my own eyes.

Aunt May reached the gate. She stood on the road that led to the huge metal doors—doors capable of opening with the single command from the guard stationed in front of her. It was a single guard seated within the operating station next to the gate, and he was staring right at May.

Afraid of being seen, I ducked behind the last rundown house before the main road. I peered around the side of the house so that only my head was visible, ready to run if trouble arose.

"Tim," Aunt May said, moving to stand directly in front of the glass box. "Thank you for doing this." The guard just looked at her, unresponsive. "Tim?" she repeated.

My ears registered the sound of wheels against pavement—multiple vehicles from the loudness of it, moving toward May from the road behind her. May spun around, her face lit up with fear.

"What did you do?" she screamed at the guard. "We trusted you!"

Three black vans came to a stop facing Aunt May, and guards poured out to surround her. I held my breath, as if any sound I made would alert the guards to my presence.

They were dressed in all black, infamous silent pistols tucked in each belt. These guns were the only weapons permitted in Oportet, and only the guards and the Council could possess them. They were said to be a special kind of gun that emitted no noise when fired. A black helmet covered the entirety of the guards' faces, the tinting so heavy that even up close their eyes were not visible.

Aunt May stood, in her beautiful red dress, her hair flying all around her as she faced a considerable display of Oportet's law enforcement. Even then, she was absolutely stunning.

The guards all took position, and I watched in horror as they pointed the silent pistols directly at my aunt's forehead, the red lasers coming together as one.

You can't kill her! I screamed in my head. It went against the central tenets of Oportet: life had meaning and it should be protected.

My feet were cemented in place, and I couldn't pull my eyes away for even a second. A final van pulled up behind the others, and I recognized Councilman Tomlinson stepping out along with two more uniformed guards.

"May Ashford," Tomlinson said, standing behind the line of guards. They parted before him, creating a gap between him and May. "I can not in good conscious call this a surprise. Your friend here made certain of that." Tomlinson gestured to the petrified guard inside the gate's command center. "I need you to come out here, Mr. Garfield."

The guard came out of the center, and Tomlinson motioned for him to stand next to May.

"But I did what you said," he sputtered as half of the guards moved their lasers to his forehead. "You said I would get my reward and come away free!"

"You sold us out for money?" May blurted, her face contorting at the magnitude of the man's treachery.

"I love how situations like this illustrate humanity's true nature," Tomlinson proclaimed. "Don't worry, you'll be free from all of this very soon."

"The rules forbid murder," May pleaded. "How can you take away a life that you profess has meaning and purpose?"

Tomlinson waved a hand dismissively to silence her. "You don't understand, do you? Your life has no meaning. Your life lost all of its meaning the day you decided to turn away from the rules. I wouldn't call this murder; that would imply that I was going to kill you. You, my dear, are already dead."

"You're insane!" said the guard next to May. "How the hell have you stayed in power for this long?"

The guards tensed at the outburst, and I was caught by surprise at his bluntness. Then I realized that if there was ever a time to question anything, it was now. There was nothing more he could lose.

"Because I understand how a successful government should operate," Tomlinson answered simply. He spoke as if he was having a casual chat with an old friend rather than a man he was planning to execute. "There needs to be enough freedom to give the people the illusion of free will, and enough control to keep the masses from questioning and thinking too much. When this balance is reached, you have a society that finds meaning in following the rules and obeying their leaders.

"A citizen will cling to these beliefs because it is only through them that he will acquire his own delusional since of self—his meaning and purpose—and only through them will he feel he is a part of the powerful whole of the society. Outsiders are hated for not having these same values and beliefs, and any freethinking is despised for its possible destruction of the previously mentioned sense of self.

"When being a dutiful citizen is all you are, and all you wish to be, it makes a leader's job quite simple. How do I censor and shelter my people from anything that might disrupt this sense of self?" Tomlinson paused, looking back and forth between May and the guard. "Do you understand?" he asked. He wore a slight smile now, a smile of pride.

"The only thing I understand is that we had a deal," the guard spat.

"I don't understand why you won't let me pass through to the Outside," May said, ignoring the man next to her. "If my life is really so meaningless, why can't I go live it outside of Oportet?" she rushed on. "You let disorderly Outsiders out of Oportet all the time," she added, her eyes pleading.

Tomlinson shook his head, the same prideful smile on his lips. "Oh, May. No reason to be so naïve. Not now."

"What are you saying?" Aunt May cocked her head. Her voice shook with fear.

"No one leaves Oportet. That isn't how it works."

His words took a moment to sink in. I sucked in a breath, thinking about Alex. He deserved a life of solitude, maybe, but death?

"We want to paint a picture of a utopia to the Outsiders, and that cannot be done with any failures. If we have a stream of people leaving this society, then it is not a utopia, now, is it?"

A look of resignation crossed May's features. She was done fighting.

"There are no other options, Ms. Ashford."

I could not tear my eyes away. I could not turn my head and refuse to witness, even as Tomlinson signaled the guards, even as tiny clicks sounded, even as my beautiful aunt fell to the ground, dead before making contact.

A scream was building in my throat, and I was powerless to stop it. Just as it made its way to my lips, a large hand clamped over my mouth.

"Shh. Don't scream. They'll kill you if you scream." A gruff voice I didn't recognize whispered in my ear. "I told her to wait. She should have waited," the man choked out.

Tears were falling down my cheeks, and the hand lifted from my mouth. My mind was too preoccupied with keeping my eyes locked on Aunt May's lifeless body as it was carried to one of the vans to even consider the stranger behind me.

My whole body trembled with rage. How dare those monsters touch my aunt like she was a meaningless shell of a person. It took all I had not to scream, fight, punch, and kick until my body and voice ached.

I owed it to May to hold myself together, to live for what she believed was right. If I died, then we would both die in vain.

"Are you Luna?" the man asked. I finally turned around to face the man who had just saved my life.

"Yes." My voice came out in a choked whisper, and I almost didn't recognize it as my own.

The man had a soft, handsome face and was dressed in a lab coat. He was wearing glasses, and his blue eyes were brimming with tears.

"Dr. Gary Reynolds," he said softly, staring into my eyes. "You look like her."

"You're the one in love with my aunt," I said. I was finally beginning to see the whole picture, and this man was the final piece. He was responsible for all of the mysterious phone calls. He was supposed to be leaving with Aunt May today.

I could not stop a strangled sob from escaping my lips, and I could feel a huge wave of sobbing and heaving building up within me. I was being torn apart.

"We have to get out of here," he said, awkwardly placing a hand on my back in an effort to comfort me.

I looked once more into the man's eyes, and I could see two reflections of myself: one was my pained face on the lenses of his glasses, and the other was in the two orbs of blue beyond them. His eyes did not contain my face as the glasses did. Rather, they contained the brokenness and all-consuming void that was eating me away inside. It was the kind of darkness that made me wonder if there was ever any light. It was the kind of emptiness that yearned for my submission. His reflection of my mind's state was making me wonder if there was anything at all to hang on to, or if everything was fated to succumb to oblivion.

I owed it all to lost hope. Oportet stripped us of our hope for something more. The something more was a nameless thing: a breath of an idea, a whisper of a thought, or a hum of spontaneous action.

It would have been so easy to look into this man's eyes and admit defeat—to do what was expected of me, and to accept the reflection of myself as I saw it—but I wanted that something more. I wanted to give it a name, and be where I could wear it for all to see. I did not want to be the girl in the reflection. I wanted to be more.

I wanted to be more than an obedient citizen. I wanted to be more than a girl who blindly followed the rules. I wanted to be more than the daughter who only held value when she did as she was told. I wanted to be more than the Council's deliberately engineered sociology project.

That was my hope. That was how I would honor Aunt May, and that was how I would escape the reflection of emptiness in Dr. Reynolds's eyes.

~~~~~

We had skirted around deteriorating houses until reaching a silver car a block from Aunt May's abandoned vehicle. I looked away, unable to even cast my eyes in the direction of the sleek, red car left by an owner who would never return.

The car and I had a lot in common. I almost found myself sympathizing with the vehicle, somehow forgetting that it was an inanimate object that lacked the capacity for emotion. That was where our similarities came to a halt. We might have both been abandoned, but I was the one who had to endure the pain that came with it.

"I'll take you home," Dr. Reynolds said gruffly.

I nodded. My brain was not producing enough coherent thoughts for me to really assess my current situation. I only had one thing on my mind: change.

I needed to stop running from change. I needed to finally admit to myself what I wanted and pursue it. I had no other options—something needed to change.

Leaving my bike behind, I slipped into the passenger's seat and recited my address monotonously. Dr. Reynolds had shielded his emotions in record time, his face now resembling a kind of stone sculpture.

"Why were you there?" he asked after a few minutes of silence.

I asked myself the same question. I had no idea what had possessed me to trail my aunt on a bicycle for three miles. Something drew me to the gates, and I had a feeling it was the same force that compelled me to keep my eyes open through the entirety of my aunt's murder.

It was the pull from within to seek the truth and to awake from the blanket of unconsciousness that covered Oportet. I trailed my Aunt because I needed to. Everything that had happened to me since August had been for a reason: Meeting and falling in love with an Outsider, defending my beliefs and choices at school, facing the darker side of humanity through Alex and the Council, receiving guidance from May, and learning what really happens to those who oppose Oportet.

It was all leading up to a final event—a final choice that would decide my eternal fate.

"She was acting strange, so I followed her," I mumbled finally.

"You were at her house?" Dr. Reynolds asked with raised eyebrows.

"Yeah. I guess she meant it to be a final goodbye," I choked out, losing it again. The tears escaping me were uncontrollable, and I almost felt embarrassed in Dr. Reynolds's stony presence.

"She loved you so much. She never stopped talking about you," he said.

I didn't feel like being comforted. It seemed like such an unbalanced exchange, a loved one's death for a bunch of meaningless words. Nothing anyone said would make any of it okay, so what was the point?

I answered Dr. Reynolds with silence, and it suited us better anyway.

We were now in front of my house, and I cast a glance in the direction of the driver's seat. Dr. Reynolds opened his mouth, but I was out of the car before he could throw at me more clichéd mutterings about my loss. My rudeness was lost to the jumbled anger, sadness and determination swirling within me.

I slammed my front door closed behind me and mindlessly moved in the direction of quiet voices. My family was sitting at the dinner table in a tense silence when I entered. Mother and Father stood at the sight of me.

"Where have you been, young lady?" Mother asked at the same time Father yelled, "How dare you disregard our wishes and miss family dinner!"

"I could care less about your family dinners right now," I snapped. I felt like I was in some kind of lucid dream. I had somewhat control of my actions amidst a completely surreal environment. Words just kept forming on my tongue, and I did little to stop them from escaping my lips.

Father started speaking, but I cut him off. "They killed her!" I screamed. "You work for—and are governed by—monsters! They're murderers! Don't you care at all?"

"Luna, you're hysterical. Go to your room and collect yourself," Mother said, her face paling with every word I uttered.

Before I could speak again, the phone began to ring. Mother moved to grab it from the wall while Father stared me down, red-faced. A vein in his forehead was protruding, and his fists were clinched at his sides.

"Hello?"

Silence.

The sound of the phone clattering to the floor seemed to resonate throughout the kitchen, all eyes returning back to me.

"It's May," Mother murmured. A cross between horror and disbelief crossed her features. "There was a car crash. She didn't make it."

Megan began to sob in my peripheral.

I shook my head violently. "Bullshit!"

"Luna!" Father roared. I had never heard him so angry. "Go to your room. You are upsetting everyone here."

"You know what's upsetting?" I asked, more composed than before.

Mother reassumed her position next to Father. Her body shook as she watched me.

"Tomlinson commanding a set of guards to gun down my Aunt," I said. "Seeing what happens to those who oppose a bunch of corrupt, brain-washing old men is what's upsetting."

"Let that be a lesson to you," Father said quietly.

My breath caught. Did he know about the executions?

"David!" Mother choked out, finally breaking through her initial shock. "May's accident had nothing to do with her misguided conspiracy theories," Mother said, hints of hysteria finally shining through the cracks of her usual contained disposition.

"Of course. My apologies, dear," Father said solemnly. "It was not my place."

I had a feeling that if Father knew anything about the executions, Mother didn't in the slightest. "Fine. Don't listen to me. It's obvious that you would rather stay comfortable than to face reality."

Mother looked at me like I was trying to convince her of the existence of fairies and unicorns, Megan was too busy letting out waves of tears to listen, and Father was too set in his loyalties with the Council to fault them for killing an unruly citizen. My family was a hopeless cause.

"Jasper," I breathed, barely emitting a sound. The weight of my actions were now fully upon me, and I had to act quickly before any damage could be done.

"What did she say?" Mother asked in between muffled sobs as I sprung into action.

I ignored the rising voices behind me as I darted for the front door. My selfishness could send Jasper to his death.

~~~~~

I pounded on Jasper's door, my fist's momentum almost causing me to punch him in the face when he answered.

Jasper caught my fist in the air, his fingers gently wrapping around it. He raised an eyebrow.

"I'm not losing my hearing, you know." He released my hand, and I let it drop to my side. "Um, come in, but I have to leave soon for that, well, you know," he stammered.

"I have to tell you something," I said, urgency evident in my voice.

Jasper led me upstairs to his room, music blasting from the stereo next to his bed. He shut it off and turned toward me, squinting at my face like there was something wrong with it. I looked away under his scrutiny.

"Have you been crying?" he asked. "What's wrong?"

We sat down on his bed and I explained everything to him—every last detail. Jasper brushed the tears from my face as I described my aunt's murder. He laced his fingers through mine when I admitted to knowing he was walking into some kind of trap, and he kissed me when I told him that we were going to find a way out of Oportet—together.

....

Chapter Twenty-Five

"**N**o," I said. "No, no, no."

"What is it? What did you remember?" Megan asked, her face contorted in pain. "You were crying and screaming, Luna."

"It wasn't crazy talk," I mumbled.

Megan scrunched her face in confusion before remembering what I was talking about. "I've begun to rethink that label," she said. "I think you know more of the truth than most people." Megan paused, her eyes wide and incredulous. "So they really did kill Aunt May, didn't they?"

I nodded.

"It's time for me to leave." I stared into Megan's eyes. "Come with me," I said, adrenaline coursing through me. This was the solution. I didn't have to feel guilty about abandoning my sister if I took her with me.

"Luna..."

"I need to get the hell out of this place, and so do you. We could live much better lives on the Outside. We could start over, Megan."

"No."

I cringed at her rejection.

"I can't go with you, Luna."

"Why?"

"I just can't. I don't want to."

"But, Megan—"

She shook her head. "It's okay, Luna. Don't feel guilty. I swear I'll be fine. But you—you need to go. I want you to be happy."

That was all I ever wanted from my family. Chills crept up my spine at the simple way Megan expressed her acceptance and love for me. It was exactly what I needed.

I wrapped her in a hug. "If I don't see you again before I leave, I just want you to know that you are an amazing little sister. I love you, Megan."

"Love you too. I hope we see each other again someday." Megan smiled softly, looking down at her feet. "Your whole life has led to this moment, hasn't it? It all fits together so perfectly."

"I think you're right. Like pieces of a puzzle." I laughed with her for a moment, and I almost lost track of all the grief surrounding my life. "Goodbye, Megan."

"Goodbye," she said, wiping a tear from her face. There had been far too many tears for one day—for one life.

I ran through my newly regained memory. First that Dr. Gary Reynolds was Aunt May's secret lover. I felt a pang of betrayal at the realization that the neurosurgeon who took my memories away was the same man who loved my aunt, *and* the same man who took me home after we watched her die.

Why would a man who performed such immoral procedures for the government plan an escape from Oportet? I just couldn't believe May was in love with such a cruel man.

Seconds later I was being slammed in the gut. The room spun. I couldn't breathe. My heart started beating dangerously fast. No air was making it to my lungs.

"Luna, stay with me." Megan's voice barely made it above the unbearable ringing in my ears. "I think you're having a panic attack or something," Megan said, peering down at me from my position on the floor.

I didn't remember falling. I rushed to my feet, clutching Megan's bedframe for support as blood rushed to my head. I wobbled for a moment, close to falling down again.

I didn't have time to utter an explanation to my frightened sister before I was forcing my feet to move across the hardwood floor.

Throwing clothing and other essentials in a bag haphazardly, I repeated my newfound safe phrase in my head: *It will all be okay.* After a while, though, it started to morph into something like: *He will be okay.*

He will be okay. He will be okay. He will be okay.

~~~~~

"Luna?" Lilly asked, letting me in and staring at me with growing curiosity.

"Can I please stay here?"

Lilly hesitated for a moment before putting a warm smile and nodding her head. "Yes. Of course, dear."

She led me to the kitchen and gestured for me to sit across from her at the table. I sat my bag down next to me, taking in a deep breath to prepare for Lilly's inevitable questioning.

"Are you alright? Has something happened?" she began.

"I'm okay." *Physically,* I added in my head. "I can't sleep under the same roof as my parents. They did something...unforgivable." I almost cringed at my own harsh language.

Lilly opened her mouth then closed it. She placed her hand over mine and squeezed.

"Honey, you have to cut us parents some slack. We all want what's best for our children, and sometimes that desire clouds our judgment."

I ignored her. "Where is Jasper? I need to talk to him."

Lilly pulled her hand away and clucked her tongue. She peered at the wall clock that hung in the kitchen. "He should've been home fifteen minutes ago. He had another meeting with Tomlinson about his—departure," she faltered. "I still can't believe he'll be on the Outside soon." Lilly put a hand on my shoulder. "Are you okay? Your face is so pale. You look sick."

Lilly's voice barely penetrated my mind. It was like a buzz in the distance, or a static television screen. How did she not know that Jasper was going to be executed?

The sound of the front door shutting pierced the room's tension. With shaking hands, I stood up from the table.

"There he is," Lilly said behind me, clearly relieved.

I focused on moving each foot forward, coming around the corner and into the foyer. Jasper had his back to me, shrugging off a dark jacket. I moved closer, my feet now audible as they moved from the carpeted area of the living room to the wood flooring of the foyer.

Jasper cast a glance over his shoulder. He fumbled with the jacket, letting it fall to the floor next to him as he turned to face me.

There was no time for thinking; there was only time for movement. Soon I was standing in front of him, noticing the deliberately disheveled hair and dark eyes so familiar to me.

I reared back and slapped the left side of his face with my open hand as hard as I could. The crack reverberated through the room like the sharp clap of thunder that follows a close lightning strike. Jasper's head snapped to the side, his cheek flushing crimson.

"You lied to me," I said, struggling to keep my shaking voice under control. "You knew this whole time that you were under a death sentence."

Jasper stared at me expressionlessly.

"You messed with my head and then left me. You knew I would eventually remember everything," I accused, my voice cracking. I took a breath and moved on. I needed to finish. "This whole time you've made me feel guilty for something beyond my control, when you were really the cruel one. You were the selfish, unfeeling one," I said, getting louder. "You were the one acting so bipolar that I couldn't tell if I was just deluding myself or if you actually wanted things to return to how they were between us.

"You kissed me knowing that soon you would be—gone, dead, whatever. Then you cut me out. What were you hoping for, Jasper?" I practically screamed. "Were you thinking that by the time I remembered how Aunt May died you would already be dead, so you wouldn't have to face me?"

Jasper's jaw was trembling. He looked away briefly, emotion finally breaking through the walls he'd built for himself. Then he met my gaze again.

"Or was this some kind of revenge for what you went through this summer? Do you really hate me that much?"

"Of course not!" Jasper exploded. "What was I supposed to do? Did you want my death sentence to be the first thing you heard from me? You would have tortured yourself for months. There was nothing you could do about it. The cruel thing would have been *to* tell you." He ran a hand through his hair.

"You're right, leading you on was a really shitty thing to do, but I just missed you so much. I thought I was finally doing the right thing when I made the break, but maybe it wasn't...hell, I don't know. This shouldn't be something an eighteen-year-old should have to deal with," he said, his eyes flashing me fear and dread in their purest forms. Jasper had known this whole time that he was *destined to die*.

I had been plotting my next words—my next digs and insults to hurl at him—but they were gone. *Jasper was going to die.*

No... No, he wasn't. I had never been surer of anything in my entire life. We would make it out. We would live.

I wrapped my arms around him, and he hugged me back. I rested my head on his chest, listening to his heart thud in my ear. We both realized how pointless it was to argue over the past. The past was nonexistent, but here—now—was teeming with life. It was teeming with hope.

"I have a plan," I said after pulling away.

Jasper took in a breath. "Let's hear it."

~~~~~

We stayed up all night ironing out the details of my intricate escape plan. We were high on the idea of resistance, of having someone—*something*—to fight for, the abstract idea I'd grasped watching Aunt May die. We were fighting for *something more.*

Determination clouded our doubt until it vanished, the fire of our passion for life and each other engulfed the pain we had become so accustomed to. We were falling in love again, and this time we wouldn't let it fall apart.

When I woke up the next morning my head was on Jasper's chest. We were both sprawled out on his bedroom floor, never having made it to the bed before sleep temporarily squelched our fire.

Wads of paper were scattered around us, and I thought I felt a notebook under my left knee. I stretched and rolled over, cringing when a pencil scraped my side.

"Ow," I moaned. I glanced over at Jasper, who was still fast asleep.

After using the bathroom, I crept back to Jasper's room as quietly as possible. I didn't want to disturb Lilly.

Just as I reached the door, a delicate hand fell on my shoulder. I jumped, spinning around.

Lilly laughed softly. "Sorry, dear. You really are jumpy, aren't you?"

I smiled. "Pretty much, yeah," I laughed.

Silence hung over us awkwardly, and I fiddled with my sleeve waiting for Lilly to speak.

"You guys are going to make it this time," Lilly whispered.

I nodded.

"Jasper finally confessed what the Council was really planning. It was also hard not to hear the truth in all that screaming earlier," Lilly said, giving me a look. She swallowed, shaking her head. "I still can't believe he would keep that from me. We got the news last week that the Council voted against him. They set the date for next Friday." Lilly shuddered. "He's known for an entire week that he was set to be executed."

"Jasper told me that he tried to get you to come with us, but you refused," I said slowly. "Why?"

"That just isn't how my life is supposed to play out. Jasper often forgets this," she explained.

"I don't understand. How can you stay here knowing what you do?"

"I came here for a reason, Luna. I knew what I was walking into." She glanced down at her feet. "My husband was shot. My child became fatherless, and I became so haunted by fear that I couldn't leave the house. I'm not haunted here."

I understood Lilly's reasons, but I could never understand why she would choose to stay in Oportet alone rather than face her demons and be free on the Outside. The thought of such a gentle, kind woman abandoned by the only person she had left to love tore me apart inside.

"You shouldn't worry about me. Actually, I won't allow it. You and Jasper were always meant to leave, and I was always meant to stay. That is just something you will have to accept. Jasper too."

I was more than frustrated at her vague attempts at blaming fate.

"I have to stay for the same reason you have to go: I'm happy here. I have found my purpose."

"I'm really going to miss you," I whispered, sighing in defeat.

"And I will miss you, my dear. I've always secretly wanted a daughter," Lilly murmured. "Take care of him, okay?"

"Always."

~~~~~

"You ready?" Jasper asked, handing me the laptop.

240

I nodded. Phase one of our master plan was starting, and knowing that we could be caught at any second was both exhilarating and terrifying.

Hacking into my father's email account was the easy part. He only used one password for all of his accounts, and I had been trusted with it on many occasions. The ten-digit number was forever etched in my brain.

The hard part was sorting through all of the pieces of Expansion Project information I had been overhearing the past few weeks. I knew that the first day of construction began tonight, and that shifts of guards and technicians were scheduled to work on it in four-hour increments.

This meant that if I posed as my father, the leader of the committee in charge of the endeavor, I could email the first shift of guards and tell them that they were being switched with the second shift. I could make up an excuse about some kind of conflict among the technicians scheduled for the second shift, like an important meeting.

The current walls will be scheduled to go down at the same time as before, but now there won't be any guards positioned by the new wall—the wall with an opening for a gate.

It would be naïve of us to think that no one would catch on to this glitch, but the plan was to sneak away before anyone had time to notice. Many things could go wrong, but Jasper and I refused to be anything less than hopelessly optimistic. At this point, we had little to lose. We had to try *something*.

"You once told me about a story called *Romeo and Juliet*," I said suddenly, looking up from the computer screen for the first time in an hour.

I had been scouring emails to find the names and emails of the first shift of guards, plus other information about how things were supposed to play out. I had to become as much of an expert as Father so I wouldn't tip off anyone with the emails I was composing. I had to write exactly like him, plus I had to include specific information vital to the Project. It had to appear real.

"Probably because that thing scarred me for life. Depressing stuff." Jasper said, munching on some popcorn Lilly made.

"Why? You said that it was a tale of forbidden love and that they were going to run away together. Did they?"

Jasper stopped throwing popcorn in his mouth and hesitated for a moment.

"Of course they did," he said. It wasn't a convincing claim.

"Then why was it depressing?"

"The two families battled, and every last one of them died," Jasper said without skipping a beat.

"Huh. That is sad," I said.

"So are you almost done?" he asked.

"I thought I was the one with impatience issues. Quit pestering me, I'm almost there."

"You should take a break," Jasper said, looking at me suggestively.

"Eat your popcorn and stop talking to me," I replied, grinning. "My will is stronger than that."

Jasper moved a Pixies CD in front of my face, putting on a pouty face like a puppy begging for food at the dinner table. He knew I didn't care for most of his rock albums.

"Fine," I said, sighing dramatically.

He slid the music into the laptop, and I emailed each guard a part of the first shift while listening to the Pixies's roller-coaster ride of mellow acoustic-backed crooning, and full-assault guitars and screaming vocals. I might never understand Jasper's love for that kind of music, but that was okay. Seeing the passion in his eyes when he talked about rock music was enough for me to love it on some level too, even if that love did not extend to listening to it.

After another hour, I shut the laptop.

"I'm done. We have a date for six o'clock," I said.

Jasper sat up. "Should I wear a tux?"

I cocked my head.

"So I could look like James Bond?" Seeing that my confusion hadn't diminished, Jasper shook his head. "Never mind. Once we reach civilization we'll have the most epic movie marathon in all of history."

I smiled at his enthusiasm.

"Seriously. It will last days, weeks even."

"Where are we going to stay?" I asked, suddenly panicked. There had been far too little thought concerning anything past our escape.

"I have tons of friends back in Portland that would help us out," Jasper said, his eyes lighting up at the change in conversation. "You'll love it there. You seem like a big-city kind of girl."

"I can't wait." I grinned, setting the laptop down on the coffee table. I leaned back next to Jasper.

"And when we get our hands on a car, I'll take you to the coast. You'll finally get to see the ocean." Jasper looked straight ahead as he spoke, already lost in the vision of our future we were dreaming up. "I do worry, though, that once you see it you'll never want to be anywhere else."

"I don't care where we go once we're out," I said. "I don't care if we never stop moving. We could drive all over the continent for all I care."

"The entire continent, huh?" Jasper paused. "Sounds epic."

"Wait, how are we even going to get to Portland?" I asked, the mental image of Jasper and I lost and dying of starvation kind of ruined all of the plans we were making.

"Well, we're going to be on bikes, and from there..." Jasper held up his thumb.

I shot him a confused look, but he just grinned.

"We're going to walk on our thumbs?" I asked, making Jasper laugh. "Wait no, we're going to use the magical properties of our thumbs to teleport ourselves?"

"Now you're just being ridiculous. Walking on our thumbs is obviously the realistic option here."

"Uh oh," I said, my vision blurring.

"What is it?"

"I'm remembering something."

Chapter Twenty-Six

···

"**S**o here's the plan," Jasper said. "You'll go home and do your best to act like everything is completely normal. You'll tell your parents that the shock of your aunt's death was just too much for you to handle. You took a walk to calm down and separate the truth from the delusions you convinced yourself to believe.

"Lilly's close friend from Portland is the guy who shuttles Outsiders in from Oportet. She just called him. He is willing to sneak us out the gate and drop us off in Portland where he's scheduled to pick up some families Monday night.

"Instead of packing our backpacks with school things, we'll pack them with essentials for the road. We'll hang out in the forest until it's time to leave at noon, and then we'll ride our bikes to the abandoned stretch of houses where the shuttle driver is meeting us. We'll duck down in the seats until we're out," Jasper finished.

"Foolproof," I said. I was ready to leave. I felt no regret; I believed I was fully capable of lying to and fighting anyone who posed a threat to our escape.

"I'll see you tomorrow morning at seven-thirty, then," Jasper said, leading me to the door.

"I'll be there. No matter what."

~~~~~

It was Sunday night. If all went as planned, Jasper and I would be on the road in less than twenty-four hours.

My parents were content enough with the fact that I came home calm and collected on Friday. I told them exactly what they wanted to hear, and although they weren't entirely convinced, it was just enough for them not to launch a full-scale investigation.

We attended a small family funeral Saturday to pay our respects to Aunt May. Megan and Mother cried. Father looked on sternly, casting me glances as if to remind me that I would end up like her if I didn't behave.

By the time of the funeral, I had no more tears to shed. I comforted Megan and hugged my mother, and that was the end of it. I knew May would be proud of me. I knew she was rooting for me from wherever she was. I made a promise to her that she wouldn't have died in vain. It was my determination to keep this promise that kept the tears at bay. Aunt May was not dead. She was alive in me.

I stirred my soup aimlessly, too busy fantasizing about what lay ahead to be bothered with my last family dinner. As soon as the words 'last family dinner' ran through my mind, the wall of apathy I had constructed for anyone but Lilly and Jasper crumbled.

My eyes flickered from face to face. Father's was stern and withered by work stress, his brown hair thinned and receded. Then I looked to Mother. Her straight red hair was tucked behind her ears as she ate, and her pale skin was dotted with freckles.

Megan was next, and she was the easiest to let past my barrier. We had been so close when we were younger. Things were different now, but I struggled with the thought of leaving her here in Oportet, where she would no doubt fade away—asleep her whole life. She looked up from her food, feeling my stare. All I saw was her bright green eyes, and the way they complemented the hair she inherited from Mother. Megan would be as beautiful as May when she was older.

"Why are you looking at me like that?" Megan asked with narrowed eyes. She giggled when I shrugged. "You're a weirdo."

"Megan." Mother shot her a look. "We don't call people names. You'll be in eighth grade in a matter of months. You'd better start acting like it."

Megan scowled and went back to eating.

I didn't want to remember my family as monsters. They weren't perfect, but their faults were mostly due to circumstance. How could I blame them for someone else's manipulation?

I wanted to remember them for the happy memories: the birthday parties, the family gatherings, the times Mother comforted me and Father made me laugh, the silly games of make-believe with Megan. I even wanted to remember Jenna as my loyal best friend of ten years.

I was leaving them. I owed them that courtesy, even if they had no way of knowing it.

"We're very proud of you Luna," Mother said, casting a glance at Father.

"For what?"

"For how hard you've worked in school all these years. We are very excited to see you graduate soon," she explained.

"Oh."

"We know you've had a rough year," Father started. He cleared his throat and took a large gulp of his water. "But I think it's finally time to put all of that behind us—for good."

I nodded. "Yes. I think so too."

Father didn't know just how literal that statement was about to be. In a matter of hours I would see Oportet in the rearview mirror, and I would be putting it behind me for good.

"Megan," Mother said. "It's your turn to wash the dishes."

Megan huffed, stacking our plates up and carrying them to the kitchen sink. My eyes followed her as she went, and then rested on the clock that hung on the wall above her. It was six forty-five.

Right on cue, the phone rang.

"That's Jenna calling about the essay," I said, rising from the table. A few hours ago I filled my parents in about an imaginary English essay, along with a scheduled phone call with who they thought was my best friend.

Mother exchanged glances with Father. I watched as her eyes moved to her laptop.

"You may be excused," Father said. "Your Mother and I have some work to do as well."

Ignoring my parents' fidgety movements and awkward glances, I rushed upstairs to grab the phone.

"Hey," I answered just as my fingers closed around the plastic. I was slightly out of breath from my sprint up the stairs.

I clicked my door shut behind me and lay back on my bed. I glanced around my room, programming each pattern of fabric and piece of furniture into my mind. I never wanted to forget anything about my room—my home. I didn't want to forget the feel of the cool wood of my desk beneath my fingers, the way the morning sun cast designs with its light against my carpet, or even how it felt to creep under my warm covers in the dead of winter. I wanted to keep it with me, even as I left it empty and lifeless without my presence.

"Any cold feet?" Jasper asked.

I snapped out of my trance at the sound of his voice.

"Nope." I would be meeting Jasper tomorrow even if my legs stopped working. I didn't mind crawling. "But that might just be because I'm wearing socks."

"Feeling witty, are we?"

"Can't we just go tonight? I don't think I can wait any longer."

"I know what you mean." Jasper sighed. "But unfortunately that bus won't get here until tomorrow."

"Yeah, I know. Seven-thirty, right?" I asked, although I was more than sure of the time. How could I forget?

"Seven-thirty. If all goes as planned, we'll be in Portland in less than twenty-four hours."

"I know. I've been repeating that fact in my head all day. We're so close," I said, looking out my window. A full moon hung in the sky, reminding me of the first time I ever spoke to Jasper on the phone. He told me that Luna was another name for the moon.

I fell asleep with the moon painted on the inside of my eyelids, giving me the courage I needed. Aunt May had chosen my name, and I imagined her watching me from the sky, taking the form of the giant, glowing orb I was named after.

~~~~~

I stared at myself in the mirror for a good ten minutes. My stomach was going crazy: nervousness, anxiety, fear and excitement bouncing about inside me.

I braided my long, dark hair and pushed it to the side to keep it out of my face. The weight of my backpack finally jolted me to the present, reminding me of the schedule I promised to keep.

It was six-thirty. I had about an hour to eat my breakfast and see my family one last time.

"I made you some tea," Mother said, setting the steaming cup next to my bowl of cereal.

"Oh, thanks."

After several, long minutes of eating with my family in silence, I carried my empty bowl to the sink, glancing at the clock. Fifty minutes, now.

I went back to the table where the family carried on with their morning routine: Megan eating waffles, Father reading the newspaper, and Mother fiddling around on her laptop. Mother periodically looked up to shoot me strange glances, as if she was making sure I was still there. Actually, the whole family was acting odd—unnatural. It was starting to make my stomach churn.

"How's the tea?" Father asked without looking up from the paper.

"Mine's good," Megan chirped, looking over at me expectantly.

Mother, trying to be subtle, peeked at my cup to see. She smiled, seemingly content that it was half-empty.

What was so important about the tea? What was going on? Warning bells were wailing in my head. They were telling me to run. It was like my subconscious knew exactly what was going on, even if I didn't. All I knew was that my family was acting unusually strange today.

"The tea is fine," I said slowly, shaking my head to let everyone know that they were freaking me out. "Well, time for me to leave."

Mother's head shot up. "Why? School doesn't start for more than an hour, and it only takes ten minutes to walk."

"Fine," I huffed. "I can wait a few more minutes if that makes you happy." I lifted my teacup to my mouth, and then set it down without taking a drink.

The doorbell rang right at seven.

"Luna," Mother said, her eyes darting to the door, to father, then back to me. "Don't fight them, sweetie."

"What are you talking about?" My breath was caught in my throat, the air seeming unusually thick. The warning bells continued to wail, getting louder and louder. "I have to go," I mumbled, my voice coming out all warped and foreign.

I stood up, having to clutch the table for support. My limbs felt tired and heavy, and my mind felt numb. I had lost control of my body. I felt like screaming, but I wasn't quite sure how to open my mouth.

My cup of tea mocked me from its place at the table, and I struggled to push myself into an upright position.

I searched Mother's eyes for an explanation, for anything, but she was looking away, unwilling to watch the results of the decision to drug her oldest child. Megan was gone, and I heard the slamming of a door following footsteps on the staircase.

I turned away, my leaded limbs moving awkwardly in slow motion. Father was talking with two guards by the open front door, and the desire to scream reemerged.

My family was having me killed. They would rather have me dead than on the Outside. But how did they know about the plan? Jasper and I had been so careful....

The sound of tiny clicks and the sight of May falling to the ground in a lifeless heap flashed before my eyes. This wasn't how it was supposed to be. I was supposed to escape. I was supposed to be free.

Then I thought of Jasper. He would be waiting for me in the forest, wondering where I was. He would think that I changed my mind, and that I didn't want to go with him anymore.

"Did you take care of the shuttle driver?" Father asked.

"He's been relieved of his position," a guard answered.

"I have to go take care of the boy," Father said, a small envelope in his left land. "Be careful with her, okay?

"Yes sir."

"No!" I screamed, somehow finding my voice. "Don't hurt him. It was all my fault, not his, just kill me!" My speech was all slurred, and I wasn't sure if anyone understood what I was saying.

Father looked at me pityingly. "You'll be okay, Luna," he said, disappearing through the doorway.

The two guards moved towards me slowly, their black helmets shielding any hint of humanity. I noticed the silent pistols stashed in their belts and sprung into action.

The first guard reached out a hand to grab my arm, and I darted away, my wobbly feet protesting against the movement.

"How much of the stuff did you give her?" the second guard asked.

"All of it," Mother said from behind me.

"Damn, she's strong," he said. "Usually they turn to mush with a full dose," the man said, his voice containing an accent I didn't recognized.

I wasn't quick enough. The guards caught up to me in a heartbeat, my foot barely making it past the doorframe. Hands tightened around each of my arms. A black van was parked in our driveway.

"It'll be alright, hon," said the guard with the unique accent. "No need to fight."

I needed to fight with all I had—so I did.

I slammed my foot into one of the guard's shin, his grip loosening slightly. I kicked the other just as hard as before, feeling the bone of his shin beneath my heel as it made impact.

Chapter Twenty-Seven

....

I opened my eyes to darkness. Jasper was holding me against him, tracing circles on my back.

"It's okay," he murmured. "They aren't taking you away this time."

I must have been voicing what was in my memory because last time I checked, Jasper did not have mind-reading abilities. I almost didn't feel embarrassed. The warmth and comfort of Jasper's arms erased it all away.

"You're okay," Jasper said, smoothing his hand down the length of my hair. "We're going to be okay."

~~~~~

"Say hello to everyone for me," Lilly said, pulling her son in for one last hug.

"I will, Mom," Jasper promised. He pulled away. "Are you sure?" he asked her, his eyes begging. He needed to make a final attempt to get Lilly to come with us.

"I'm sure," Lilly affirmed, smiling through tears. She pulled me in for a hug, kissing the top of my head. "Stay safe," she whispered.

The walls were going down at six. We had twenty minutes to ride our bikes to the edge of town.

"Are you ready?" Jasper asked me, searching my eyes.

"I'm ready."

~~~~~

I kept my eyes on the road in front of me, every once in a while glancing back at Jasper like there was a chance he might've sunk into the ground.

The houses we passed all started looking the same; they all were the same. They each contained people with the same ambitions, emotions, thoughts, behaviors—they were all copies living out the same lives in different bodies.

To my left a child ran about in the grass, his parents waving their arms around wildly in an argument. In twenty years, that child would become another copy—a copy of his parents, his teachers, his peers, his coworkers—and then he would make sure his children grew up to become copies of himself.

He would tell himself that he was unique. He would tell himself that he was living the right way. He would tell his kids not to question. He would tell himself not to question.

Another generation of zombies.

In the split second the child met my eyes, I wished more than anything that he would be an exception. I wished he would be like me instead of his parents. I wished he would find a way out, and help others to get out.

I felt guilty. I was leaving behind so many people—so many copies—all without a fighting chance.

What Lilly said earlier finally made sense to me. She told me that she was always meant to stay, and that I was always meant to go. She told me that I would have to accept that.

I had to accept my role. My role wasn't to wake Oportet up; I had to leave that job to someone else. That had never been my purpose, and it never would be. I was meant to escape, to send a message, even if that message only reached a handful of people. My family, my friends, the Council—they would all hear it loud and clear.

Just as our bikes came to a halt in front of the massive wall, a deafening mechanical noise erupted. The wall was going down.

"How poetic," Jasper said from beside me.

I smiled. "Isn't it?"

We watched as the wall began to sink. Other than the technician manning the operation, we were probably the only citizens watching the spectacle in all its glory. The Council had ordered everyone to retreat indoors right at six.

It took what seemed like ages for the wall to recede all the way into the ground, and I was starting to get paranoid. Jasper shot me a look, noticing how many times I glanced over my shoulder in the past two minutes.

"Luna, look."

I turned, gasping as I took in the vast stretch of land ahead of us. There was only one road already built, and it was right in front of us.

"You were unbelievably accurate," Jasper said.

"I did scour through a million emails, didn't I? It only seems logical I would find out where the road to the new gate would be."

Jasper sucked in a deep breath. "So this is really happening," he said, running a hand through his hair.

"Cold feet?" I asked jokingly.

"I'm wearing socks," Jasper said, grinning.

It was almost a year ago that we had that phone conversation, the phone call that was tapped by my parents. That phone call nearly cost us everything.

"Let's go." I needed to get out of Oportet as soon as possible.

We got back on our bikes and pedaled down the road. We talked about nothing but the future—places we wanted to visit, things we wanted to do, the kind of houses we wanted to live in—they were all fair game.

I was going to be a writer and he was going to be a musician. When we got bored of one city, we would move to the next.

"Did you hear that?" Jasper asked after ten minutes of riding.

"What?" I asked, my heart speeding up.

"I don't know...I guess it was nothing. Never mind."

"Okay."

It wasn't nothing; it was something. It was the sound of tires on pavement.

"Get off the bikes or get bullets in your heads," commanded a voice behind us. It sounded like a guard speaking through a megaphone.

I looked over at Jasper, whose face had hardened, the light that was in his eyes just moments ago darkening. We obeyed, sliding off of our bikes and facing the two vehicles of guards behind us.

The guards filed out, moving into a formation similar to the one they used to gun down Aunt May. Jasper and I turned to each other, paling as we took in the red dots positioned on our foreheads.

Right on cue, Tomlinson slid out of the second van just as each guard had fallen into place. I knew how this ended. So did Jasper. He intertwined his fingers with mine.

My breath caught as another figure emerged from the car. It was Dr. Reynolds, in the same lab coat and glasses he wore last spring. He was going to watch us die just as he watched May die. Her death must have changed him.

When I saw the emptiness in his eyes, and when I decided I wouldn't succumb to that same void, Dr. Reynolds had lost his hope. I wondered if he even recognized me.

Tomlinson turned and shook the doctor's hand. "Thank you for your service to Oportet," he said. "We wouldn't have stopped them in time without you."

Dr. Reynolds looked straight at me, and I greeted him with a venomous glare. He was why Jasper and I would never make it out of Oportet. He was why we were about to die.

"It was my duty, as a citizen," Dr. Reynolds said, never tearing his eyes away from mine.

"Let's make this quick," Tomlinson muttered. "We'll have to tell her family that she and the boy made it out. I wouldn't expect them to rebel, but we'd better play it safe."

Tomlinson moved to stand behind the five guards, and Dr. Reynolds remained a few feet behind them all, his hands in his pockets.

"I love you, Luna," Jasper whispered low enough so that I was the only one who heard. "This is my fault. You would be eating dinner with your family right now if I hadn't screwed everything up."

"Jasper, I swear to God, don't even go there," I snapped. "I love you too, you idiot." I gave his hand a slight squeeze. "No regrets."

"No regrets," he echoed.

"Luna Beckham, you're quite a fighter," Tomlinson said. "I have no idea how you've managed to pull it off. You just keep building yourself up from nothing, like a phoenix rising from the ashes. It's a shame you chose the wrong side. You would have made a strong ally."

"I'd sooner die," I spat.

"It seems you've already made that decision, haven't you?" Tomlinson shook his head, laughing dryly. "What a waste." Tomlinson raised his hand, signaling the guards to prepare themselves. I only had seconds to live.

I locked eyes with Jasper. I wanted him to be the last thing I saw.

Everything fell silent but a series of five clicks: a click for each guard. My eyes shut tight. A body fell, but it wasn't mine.

Chapter Twenty-Eight

....

"**S**hit, she's got a kick, doesn't she?" the accented guard said through clinched teeth.

"Hey, grab her!" was the last thing I heard before I went tumbling down the porch stairs.

My head collided with the last step, and I felt hot liquid pool around the spot of impact. My vision blurred, and it wasn't long before I couldn't see anything at all.

~~~~~

"Set her on the table."

My eyes flew open, and I caught sight of Dr. Reynolds looking at me with concern as my body was moved by the guards to a flat surface. My head hurt. I closed my eyes again, the brightness of the room too much for me to handle.

"Can you still perform the procedure?" a voice that sounded like Mother's asked.

"It's still doable. I need everyone to leave the operating room now. She'll be moved to room one-eleven for recovery. I'll send someone for you as soon as I'm done."

I tried to lift an arm, but it was weighted in place. I did the same with all of my limbs. None of them felt connected to my body anymore.

"Luna," Dr. Reynolds whispered in my ear. "I'm going to help you. When you remember this, and you will remember this, you have to know that I would never hurt you. You will remember everything," he said.

I had not a clue what this crazy man was trying to say, where I was, or what procedure everyone was talking about.

"When you remember, you'll have to keep it a secret. Don't trust anyone. No one can know you remember."

Chapter Twenty-Nine

"The notes," I whispered to myself. Dr. Reynolds wrote the notes. *Don't trust anyone.*

My eyes flew open at the realization I'd returned to the present, the hand that once held Jasper's now empty.

At my feet lay five dead guards. Five clicks: a click for each guard.

"She's fine, just remembering something," Jasper said to my left. "We can tell you about that on the road." There was a shuffling sound, then something like a body being kicked. "What are you going to do with him?"

I spun around to see Tomlinson on the ground, his hands held out in front of him. Dr. Reynolds, with a silent pistol in hand, stood next to Jasper.

"Avenge my fiancée," Dr. Reynolds replied, looking at Tomlinson like he was a spider crawling up his arm.

"That was the last memory," I said softly. "It's over."

Jasper glanced over at me, his eyes widening when he realized that I was back for good. I had finally recovered all that was taken from me.

Jasper rushed over to me, and I met him halfway. He cupped my face in his hands, pulling it to his. His lips moved against mine, demanding, loving, and most of all—relieved.

Click.

We pulled apart, and I caught sight of Tomlinson falling, lifeless, over Jasper's shoulder. Jasper moved to shield me from the sight, but it was too late.

I had witnessed far too much death for one lifetime.

"Time to go," Dr. Reynolds said. He stuck his silent pistol back in the pocket of his lab coat, lifting his glasses to rub his eyes.

Jasper and I slid into the second row of seats, never once breaking contact. We clung to each other like it was the only way we knew how to live. The thought of our lives ending on that road changed us; we would never be the same.

The car lurched forward, slamming my head back against my seat.

"He drives like you, Jasper," I said, letting out a surprised burst of laughter. We sped down the road, and we finally caught sight of the opening in the wall ahead of us. "Dr. Reynolds?"

"Yes?"

"Thank you," I said. I saw him nod in the rearview mirror, the corners of his mouth tipping upwards. After a moment of silence, my curiosity won me over. "So how did you know where we were?"

"One of the guards from the first shift contacted your father, asking him a question about the nature of his duties, and imagine his surprise when the guard mentioned how glad he was to be moved to the second shift rather than the first. That's when he called me—your family had kept in contact with me since the procedure, and they trusted me." He shrugged.

"Your father explained the situation to me. He said that you had no doubt run off to your boyfriend's house, and that he feared you were planning an escape. He told me about the suspicions concerning your remembrance, and it didn't take long for all the signs to add up. I hadn't realized that they also called the first shift of guards and Tomlinson, alerting them to go to the new wall immediately. I asked Tomlinson if I could go along for the ride, and he agreed; I'm also highly respected among the Councilmen for my innovations in neuroscience technology. Tomlinson had no reason to doubt me," he finished.

"We owe our lives to you," Jasper said, his arm still around me. "I'm not sure if that debt can ever be repaid."

"You helped me get out of Oportet and avenge the murder of my fiancée," Dr. Reynolds said simply. "Consider yourselves no longer indebted."

I swallowed. I knew that Jasper and I wouldn't be alive if it weren't for Dr. Reynolds and his silent pistol, but I hated that more death was our only option. I couldn't say I felt incredibly guilty for the death of a murderer—who knew how many executions Tomlinson had ordered in his lifetime?

The opening for the gate grew bigger and bigger in the horizon until we sped through it. We must have been going at least eighty miles per hour.

The three of us cheered and yelled like maniacs. Jasper and I kissed. Dr. Reynolds hurled his silent pistol out the window. The storm was over; the skies were clearing.

By the time the sun disappeared behind the massive trees, Jasper had fallen sound asleep, his head resting on my shoulder as I watched the world speed by outside my window.

The moon was full and big, and the way it was sending light through my veins let me know that the hardest part of my life was over. It was finally time to discover that *something more*.

Epilogue

....

Dear Megan,

I just wanted to send you another update. I miss you. I keep thinking I see you around Portland, but it's always just some other red-haired preteen.

It has been almost three years since I left you, and I have spent every day learning and growing. I did exactly what I said I would do. I found my purpose through traveling and writing. I always thought I would write fiction, like the stories Aunt May used to read us, but as it turns out, I suck at fiction.

So I wrote my story. I started at the beginning and wrote all the way through my escape. I learned to accept that my purpose was not to wake up those in Oportet, but that didn't mean I couldn't open the eyes of those on the Outside.

I don't call them Outsiders anymore, and I don't use the term "the Outside" unless I'm writing to you. Everyone is so different here. I like it...well, until the fighting breaks out. There is always someone feuding with someone else, through words or actions, it doesn't really matter. Their differences tear them apart. It's still better than being all the same, I suppose. I still don't understand why it's so hard to tolerate the differences. Maybe I have a different perspective—considering where I've come from and what I've been through.

Not everyone fights. People are starting to learn how to cooperate and live without a government, and that's scary for them. Everyone was so used to their old methods of division, but I think they are finally learning the concept of unity.

All of ~~Jasper's~~ our friends are really cool. I wish you could meet them.

I've started something, Megan. The ~~Outsider's~~ people here are letting go of their fear. There was a protest in front of Oportet's headquarters in Portland (where Outsiders apply to become citizens). There were people screaming into megaphones, reading excerpts from my book. Some handed out flyers and held up big signs. I had never seen anything like it before! The people here are so passionate when it comes to what they believe to be wrong. They aren't afraid to speak out. Jasper says it wasn't always like that. He says that just before the fall of the American government, protesting was essentially illegal. He said that if you protested against the powerful, you could be labeled a terrorist.

The people have learned how to stand up for themselves again. They have learned what it means to change people—to change themselves—when something isn't right.

Jasper calls me a celebrity, which means I'm "adored by the masses," as he puts it. He likes to exaggerate.

I heard that the number of people applying to become citizens of Oportet is down more than eighty percent since my book became a bestseller. So much for the Expansion Project, now there won't be anyone to fill up the new space. Ha!

Jasper and I don't care too much for the glory or fame, though. We're happy just sharing our story. Jasper's in a band now, did I tell you that? People love him. I guess you could call him a celebrity too!

We moved into an apartment in Portland. Jasper was right. I am a big-city girl. It's nice to take a break from all of the traveling and settle in one spot for a while, you know?

Well, I guess that pretty much sums up our lives for now. I hope I see you again someday, Megan. I hope you learn how to speak out. I hope you find love. Love for what you do, and love for how you live.

I hope you change a life. It doesn't matter if it's just one. It doesn't matter if all you do is change yourself. Maybe you already have.

I hope that you learn to think and act differently than the rest of them. I hope you make people look twice. I hope you make people think twice.

I hope that you reach high. I hope that you see yourself in others, and I hope that this makes you a kinder person.

I hope you don't stop doing all of these things until you're happy. I hope that you find what I did: the flame that ignites within you when you find out what it is that you love, the light that enters your eyes when you tell people about it, and the soaring feeling when you see something through to the end.

I hope you learn to feel, to experience, to try anything once—to stop and think before you speak or act—to question everything.

Above all, I hope that you learn to trust yourself.

I know that you've been told your whole life that trusting yourself and questioning things is dangerous. I know that you're scared. I was once scared, too.

I hope you let go of that fear.

Be courageous.

Be spontaneous.

That is all I ask of you. I know it's a lot.

I also know that this letter will be stashed away in the second drawer of my dresser with all the other letters.

Maybe you'll get to read them one day.

With love,

Luna

Get the News

....

Thank you for reading Awaken. To hear the minute I release a new book, sign up for my free newsletter at http://maggiesunseri.com.

Acknowledgements

I would like to first thank my supportive parents for helping me make my dream a reality. I never could've done this without them. To my mom I owe the most thanks, for not only has she been my biggest fan, she has also tirelessly edited, formatted and promoted my book. I need to offer thanks to my dad, who also read Awaken, and then read it again, to provide his edits and suggestions that greatly improved the story.

I also have my encouraging and inspiring teachers to thank. Mrs. Gibson and Mrs. Joyner, you have helped me improve and grow as a writer this year. You have also given me generous amounts of encouragement. To all of my other amazing teachers over the years, you as well deserve my gratitude for pushing me and helping me develop as a writer and a person.

A special thanks to all of the friends and family members who have ever encouraged me to pursue my dreams, no matter how crazy they seemed. Lelia Graf, you have been my best cheerleader through all of this. I am so thankful for someone who so avidly motivated me to get this story out there.

Finally, I'd like to throw a thank you out into the universe for every writer, poet, artist, musician, activist or anyone else who has ever influenced me. What you bring into this world inspires me, makes me think, and shapes my perception of our world. Ideas *can* change the world. Words *do* have power.

About the Author

....

Awaken is Maggie Sunseri's first novel. She lives with her family in central Kentucky. Aside from her passion for reading and writing, Maggie enjoys documentaries, cooking and nutrition, and the practice of mindfulness. Her dystopian fiction stems from her interest in history, politics, and contemporary activism movements such as environmentalism, animal rights, and gender equality.

She would love to hear from you!

Maggie Sunseri
P.O. Box 1264
Versailles, KY 40383

Web site: http://maggiesunseri.com
Email: authormaggiesunseri@gmail.com
Facebook: https://www.facebook.com/authormaggiesunseri
Twitter: @MaggieSunseri

19446759R00165

Made in the USA
Middletown, DE
21 April 2015